CW00350711

GHOST L_ _ _ _ _

Also by Pierre Drieu la Rochelle

The Man on Horseback

GHOST LIGHT

Le Feu Follet

PIERRE DRIEU LA ROCHELLE

ISBN: 978-1-954357-06-8

Cover photograph courtesy of Fortepan / Lissák Tivadar

This translation is dedicated to the memory of J.T.
Requiescat in pace.

Introduction

Le Feu Follet is by far the most well-known work of Pierre Drieu la Rochelle in the English-speaking world, largely because of Louis Malle's film version from 1963 starring Maurice Ronet. The book was first translated by Richard Howard in 1965 as *The Fire Within*, and then again by Martin Robinson as *Will O' The Wisp* in 1966, making this present volume its third English version. In contrast, most of Drieu's other works remain untranslated.

This new translation also carries a new title. "*Feu follet*" is the French term for a natural phenomenon that occurs over bogs and swamps at night, a kind of illusory light. As a literary metaphor it carries much the same meaning as a desert mirage—something which leads one on with a false sense of hope, unattainable because it isn't real. The English term is "will o' the wisp," but this is no longer in common use, probably a reflection of our increasing disconnect from nature. "The Fire Within" is an appealing phrase, but does not carry the meaning of the original title—*follet* means "manic," not "within." Furthermore it is somewhat misleading because the book is concerned precisely with the absence of an inner fire in the lives of its characters.

Ghost Light is a vitalist writer's portrait of the absence of vitality. It is the story of the last day in the life of a heroin addict as he reflects back on the life he has led. Drieu published the book in 1931 after his involvement with the Surrealist movement in France, and it is based on the life of someone he knew, the poet Jacques Rigaut, who committed suicide in 1929.

Like Julius Evola, Drieu was at first drawn to the avant-garde art movements of the early 20th century for their attempted radicalism, their rejection of rationalism and materialism in favor of the unconscious and the suprarational, and their decidedly anti-bourgeois ethic. However, he soon found these movements to be a dead end, leading most of their adherents to eventually become lost either in Eastern mysticism or in communism to try to escape the pervasive meaninglessness that infects modern society.

Drieu would follow another path, becoming a dedicated fascist in 1934 and remaining one until the end of his life, in 1945. He sought in fascism —and, at first, thought he had found in it—a remedy for the problem which preoccupied him more than any other: the problem of decadence.

Ghost Light is a tragic tale of a young man who senses, acutely and painfully, the emptiness of modern life, and the desire within himself to live another way, to have something more, but who can find no path, no outlet for his energies. It is also a criticism of the ethos of liberal society as it existed in France at that time—its permissiveness and laziness, in which young men squander their energies in foolish and meaningless pursuits, only to realize later, when it is already too late, that they might have become something else, something better.

But while Drieu has compassion and understanding for his protagonist Alain, *Ghost Light* is not a tale of pity and excuses. The defects in Alain's character—in his psychology and even his physiology—which contribute to his downfall are laid bare with a ruthless honesty that reflects Drieu's deep and clinical understanding of modern decadence.

However, there is also a certain nobility in Alain, or at least an aspiration to it, which is absent in the novel's other characters, and which Drieu honors in his portrayal. Despite the defects and shortcomings in his character, there is a kind of incisive objectivity in Alain's assessment of both the world around him and of himself. If we cannot commend or condone his final decision, it is nonetheless true that none of the other characters possess the same intensity or honesty.

Although written nearly a hundred years ago, the book is as relevant now as it was then. The same empty distractions which consume the life of Alain—chasing after money, and the fleeting pleasures of drugs and sex—are still the things vaunted as the greatest goods by a society that no longer has any concept of higher values. Moreover, we have come to have a not-very-subtle admiration for suicides, especially artists—Ian

Curtis, Kurt Cobain—who are thereafter lauded by the media as though their work had been bestowed with a new profundity.

Ghost Light is a hauntingly beautiful book, with a vivid immediacy seldom found in literature. Its tragedy should be read as a diagnosis and a warning.

ROGUE SCHOLAR PRESS
APRIL 2021

Appearance is for me the active and living itself, which goes so far in its self-mockery as to allow me to feel that there is nothing here but appearance and will o' the wisp and a flickering dance of spirits ...

Thus spoke the iron to the magnet: 'I hate you most, because you attract me, but are not strong enough to draw me towards you.'

NIETZSCHE

PIERRE DRIEU LA ROCHELLE

One

At that moment, Alain studied Lydia intensely. But then he had been scrutinizing her ever since she had arrived in Paris three days earlier. What was he looking for? A sudden realization about her, or about himself.

Lydia was looking at him too, her eyes dilated but lacking intensity. And soon she looked away, and, closing her eyes, became absorbed. In what? In herself? Was it her self, this rumbling, satisfied anger that swelled her neck and belly? It was only the mood of a moment. It was already gone.

So he stopped looking at her too. For him, the sensation had slipped away, like a snake between two stones, eluding him once again. He remained motionless for a moment, lying on top of her; but tense, propped up on his elbows, not abandoning himself. Then, as his flesh lost its power, he felt useless, and rolled over beside her. She was lying almost on the edge of the bed; he had just enough room to lay on his side, close to her, above her.

Lydia opened her eyes again. All she saw was a hairy chest, no head. She didn't care: she hadn't experienced anything very violent either, but something had clicked, and that sensation, shallow but clear, was all she had ever known.

The dim light, which shimmered in the bulb on the ceiling, barely revealed unknown walls or furniture through the scarf which Alain had wrapped around it.

"Poor Alain, how uncomfortable you look," she said after a moment, and without hurrying, she made room for him.

"A cigarette," she asked.

"It's been a long time …," he whispered in a blank voice.

He reached for the pack which he had taken care to put on the nightstand when they'd gone to bed a few minutes before. It was a full pack, but the third of the day. He tore it open with his fingernail and they both experienced pleasure—as though they had been deprived of it for a long time—in pulling out the two small white rolls, well stuffed with fragrant tobacco.

Without bothering to turn her head, she leaned back and, twisting her beautiful shoulders, blindly searched for her purse on the other nightstand, from which she pulled a lighter. The two cigarettes burned. The ceremony was over, they had to talk.

But that no longer bothered them as it used to; no longer afraid to reveal themselves, each one was at the point of finding the being of the other already lacking, but still enjoyable: they had slept together perhaps a dozen times.

"I am happy to see you again, Alain, for a moment alone."

"I'm afraid I've spoiled your visit."

PIERRE DRIEU LA ROCHELLE

He was not trying to apologize for what had happened. And she didn't blame him; as long as she had come to him she was in danger of such incidents. However, wasn't she making a little secret effort to persuade herself that over three days in Paris, with Alain, she would have to spend one at police headquarters, after being picked up with him in a den of drug addicts?

"Of course, you're leaving this morning," he added, in a voice slightly veiled with spite.

She was leaving on the *Leviathan*, on which she had arrived. But to do that, she had had to phone all the previous evening, because she had not reserved her return seat in New York, even though she had declared then that she would only stay in Paris a few days. Was it negligence, or a secret idea to stay? In this case, it was undoubtedly the police incident that had made her decide to leave, that night spent on a chair in the middle of detectives who smelled strongly and smoked in her face, while Alain assumed a fallen air that had surprised her. Despite her American citizenship and prompt intervention, the humiliation had lasted several hours.

Still, she was obstinate.

"Alain, we must get married."

To tell him that was her reason for taking the *Leviathan* in the first place.

Six months earlier, a young divorcée, she had gotten engaged to Alain one evening in a bathroom in New York. But three days later, she had married another, a stranger, from whom she separated soon after.

"My divorce will be pronounced soon."

"I can't say the same of mine," Alain replied with a slightly affected nonchalance.

"I know you still love Dorothy."

It was true, but that didn't stop his desire to marry Lydia.

"But Dorothy isn't the woman you need anymore, she doesn't have enough money and she lets you run around. You need a woman who won't leave you alone for a second; otherwise you get too depressed and you're ready to do anything."

"You know me well," laughed Alain.

His eyes brightened for a moment.

He was still amazed that a woman would want to marry him. For years, getting hold of a woman had been his dream; it meant money, shelter, the end of all the difficulties that made him shudder. He had had Dorothy, but she didn't have enough money, and he hadn't known how to keep her. Could he keep this one? Did he even have her now?

"I never stopped wanting to marry you," she continued, in a tone without excuse or irony. "But I had this complication that delayed me."

For years, she had lived in a world where it was understood that nothing should be explained, nor justified, where everything was done on a whim.

According to the same rules, Alain could not smile.

"You must come to New York and finish with Dorothy, or you risk getting back with her. We'll get married there. When can you leave? When will you be cured?"

She always spoke in the same even tone, without expressing any ardor. And she didn't care at all to read Alain's face; she was smoking, lying on her back, while Alain, leaning on one elbow, looked beyond her.

"I already am."

"But if the police had not arrived at that house, you would have smoked."

"No. You might have; I would have watched you."

"You think so? In any case, you went to take some heroin in the men's room at the restaurant."

"No, going to the restroom is just an old habit of mine."

It was true that Alain had not taken drugs again; but going to the toilets had always been an alibi for him to justify his perpetual absence.

"And then, Alain, they say that the cure never really works."

"You know I don't want to die from drugs."

The answer was terribly vague; but Lydia never asked questions and never expected answers.

"When we're married we'll take a trip to Asia," she said contentedly.

Some excitement seemed the way to make things better.

"Yes, to Asia or China."

She smiled. She straightened up and sat on the edge of the bed.

"Oh! Alain, dear, it's broad daylight, I must go back to the hotel."

An unspeakable element flowed through the curtains.

"Your train isn't until ten o'clock."

"Yes. But I have loads of things to do. And then I have a friend to see."

"Where?"

"At the hotel."

"She'll be asleep."

"I'll wake her up."

"She'll curse you."

"It doesn't matter."

"Let's go."

But as he was about to get up, he felt a qualm or a fear.

"Come here into my arms, again."

"No, dear, it was very good, I'm satisfied. But kiss me."

He gave her a kiss serious enough to make her want to stay in Paris.

"I love you in a very special way," she said slowly, finally looking at Alain's handsome, emaciated face.

"Thank you for coming."

He said this with that discreet emotion that he sometimes gave a glimpse of, and whose unexpected manifestation suddenly attached people to him.

But, as usual, he gave in to an absurd impulse of modesty or elegance and jumped out of bed. So she did the same, and disappeared into the bathroom.

While she removed the seal of her sterility from the innermost part of her belly and performed a brief ablution, the mirror reflected, without her taking any interest in it, her beautiful legs, beautiful shoulders, and a face exquisite but which seemed anonymous from being pale, and stupid from a borrowed coldness. Her skin was the leather of a luxury suitcase, strong, dirty, and well-traveled. Her breasts were forgotten emblems. She wiped herself off, spreading her thighs where the muscles were softening a bit. Then she went back to the bedroom to get her purse.

Alain was walking up and down, smoking another cigarette. She took another one too. Alain looked at her, without seeing her much; as was his old habit, he looked around this hotel room to discover a funny and no doubt poignant detail. But this place, where cattle paraded through without interruption, was more common than a urinal, there wasn't even any graffiti. There were only stains, on the walls, on the carpet, on the furniture. One guessed other stains on the sheets, masked by the chemistry of laundering.

"Can't you find anything?"

"No."

This body of Alain, holding a cigarette, was a ghost, even more hollow than Lydia's. He had no belly and yet the bad fat on his face made him look bloated. He had muscles, but lifting a weight would have seemed incredible. A beautiful mask, but a wax mask. The abundant hair looked false.

Lydia had returned to the bathroom to paint, over her dead face, a strange caricature of life. White on white, red, black. Her hand was shaking. She observed, without fear or pity, the subtle decay which put its cobwebs at the corners of her mouth and her eyes.

"I like these dirty hotels," she cried to Alain, "they are the only places in the world that I find intimate, because I have never gone to them except with you."

"Yes," he sighed.

He liked her because she only said necessary things. He saw, moreover, that this necessity was thin.

She was in the bedroom again. She was holding her purse in her hand, searching for a checkbook, then a pen, while looking at Alain. Her gaze expressed a sharp complacency, but without hope. She put one foot on the bed and wrote on her knee. This nudity, rudely stripped of all coquetry, could not be arousing.

She handed him a check. He took it and looked at it.

"Thank you."

He expected this money with confidence, and last night he had spent all that was left of the two thousand francs she had given him when she arrived in Paris. Now she had written: 10,000. But he owed 5,000 to the sanitarium and 2,000 to a friend who had supplied drugs. Formerly he would have thought it miraculous to be given ten thousand francs all at once, but now it was a wasted effort. Lydia was richer than Dorothy, but not rich enough. Alain's exasperated poverty created an increasingly enormous void which could only have been filled by a large fortune, one that one does not meet every day.

He smiled sweetly at her.

"I'm getting dressed, Alain, dear."

He picked up his scattered clothes and went in his turn to the bathroom.

A little later they went downstairs. The hallways were empty; they felt the heavy, universal sleep behind the doors. A disheveled and livid maid tore herself from an armchair where she was curled up snoring and opened the door for them. As Alain had given all the money he had left to the taxi that had brought them there, he quickly untied his wristwatch and gave it to her. The woman was roused from her stupor; yet she gave him a look of annoyance, for she had no lover to whom she could give this gift.

It was November, but it wasn't very cold. Day slipped over night like a wet rag on a dirty tile. They went down the Rue Blanche, between the garbage boxes filled with offerings. Lydia walked in front, her tall shoulders straight, on heels of clay. In the gray of dawn, her make-up left a feverish spot here and there.

They arrived at the Place de la Trinité. The bistro on the corner of Rue Saint-Lazare was open; they went in. The working people gathering their strength inside looked for a moment with knowing pity on this handsome, defeated couple. They drank two or three coffees, then they left.

"Alain, let's walk a little more."

He nodded. But the Chaussée-d'Antin seemed discouraging to him, and suddenly he called a taxi which was rolling along like a ball over a haunted billiard table. She frowned; but he seemed so depressed that she curbed her protest:

"I can't take you to the train," he said in a somewhat hoarse voice, slamming the door. "If I'm not at the sanitarium by eight, the doctor will kick me out."

He was sincerely sorry. She did not doubt it, for no man was as attentive as he to all the little ceremonies of feeling.

"So come to New York, Alain, as soon as you can. I will send you money; I regret not having more today. I am sure that what I have given you cannot be enough for you. And we will get married. Kiss me."

She gave him a mouth pure in line, but which felt like the bitter night. He kissed her gallantly. What a beautiful face despite the make-up, the fatigue, a certain convention of pride. She might

PIERRE DRIEU LA ROCHELLE

have loved him, but she had probably been scared off, for good this time.

Suddenly he realized he was going to be alone, and, leaning back in the taxi, he let out a loud moan.

"What is it, Alain?"

She took hold of his hand, as if hope had seized her. Their resigned coldness, their quiet affectation cracked.

"Come to New York. But I have to go back."

Alain did not want to shout: Why are you leaving? However, he knew full well that she had no good reason. She, for her part, was decidedly too weak to save Alain from what she had always been told was his fate.

They arrived at the hotel. He jumped out onto the sidewalk, rang the doorbell and kissed her hand. She looked at him again with large, diluted blue eyes spread over her cheeks. This poor charming boy, to leave him was to hand him over to his most terrible enemy, himself, it was to abandon him to this gray dawn in the Rue Cambon—with the mournful trees of the Tuileries at the end. But she took refuge in the decision she had made as a precaution: to stay only three days in Paris. As for Alain, he pursed his lips, stiffened and finally wished that she would remain locked in her narrow type of pretty woman, ignorant of even that which she loved. And so this dawn would remain gray, there would never be any sun.

"To Saint-Germain," he murmured in a tired voice to the taxi driver, as the heavy hotel door closed behind an ankle as thin and fine as silk.

The taxi took him, drowsy and frozen, to the sanitarium of Doctor de la Barbinais.

Two

Alain did not come down from his room until lunchtime.

The dining room, the lounge, the corridors, the stairs, were lined with literature. Under the eyes of the neurasthenics whom he treated, Doctor de la Barbinais had lined up portraits of all the writers who for two centuries had made themselves famous by their sorrows. With the innocent perversity of the collector, he made them gradually pass from the solid faces of the dreamers of the 19th century to those very worn out faces of certain contemporaries. But, for him as for his guests, it was only a question of celebrity. For Alain, it could have been something else; but he saw himself there in one of those museums in which he never set foot, and so he passed by very quickly.

Everyone was already at table around the doctor and Madame de la Barbinais. These shared meals seemed to Alain the most incredible moment of his stay in a place that united the equally horrible characters of the nursing home and the boarding house.

He was forced to look at the faces surrounding the table. They were not fools, only weak: the doctor had assured an easy clientele.

Mademoiselle Farnoux smiled at Alain with a meager longing. Farnoux, Farnoux Steel, cannons and shells. She was a little girl between forty and sixty, bald and wearing a black wig on her bloodless head. Born of old parents, so puny, so poor in substance, she lived in the midst of her millions in incurable poverty. From time to time, she came to Doctor de la Barbinais for a respite from the increasingly exquisite fatigue, not of living, but of watching others live. Raised with a silver spoon in her mouth, she had learned early to conserve her energy; nonetheless, she had to stop every three months, exhausted, and put herself in the tomb temporarily. In the moments when she pretended to live she was, it is true, feverishly agitated. Escorted by a huge chauffeur, who carried her from salon to salon, and a humiliated old secretary who gave her her enemas and stamped her correspondence, she traveled around Europe, to decorate herself with all the celebrities and nibble at them. She was hungry for vitality; what little she had was concentrated in one effort, that of discovering more in others. Although her temperament inclined towards mawkishness, she despised whatever resembled her, and so imposed herself upon the most dazzling natures. In front of a Russian writer with the fists of porters, she stifled a little cry, wounded in the guts, but she clung to this mass of flesh soaked in blood.

A distant but throbbing taste still threw her towards other avenues besides those of glory. She carried a germ of lust that hadn't been able to blossom and that stirred in her brain like a dead seed. She could not be satisfied with the spectacle given by her driver, a pederast who flexed his heavy shoulders at the appearance of any young man, nor with the honeyed and moreover purely allusive touches of her poor servant; she had to circle with tiny smiles and ignominious glances around all the beings who had some gifts of seduction and traded in them.

She was stung by her eternal regret in front of Alain, whom she had long ago made to tell of his bitter good fortunes in those shady lounges where she could rub elbows with all types of sordid characters.

In her other neighbor, the Marquis d'Averseau, was apparently the most complete set of everything she was fond of: a fine name, since he was descended from Marshal d'Averseau; a literary title, since he had written a *History of the French Princes who were Sodomites*; and finally, a place in the chronicle of minor scandals. But he was hideous; he would have had to be a genius to compensate for those green teeth under swollen and poisonous lips. And his anecdotes about Toulon were stale.

Beyond Monsieur d'Averseau, it was Mademoiselle Cournot, who, no less than Mademoiselle Farnoux, ogled Alain. She was huge and skeletal. Despite the best efforts of her father, Baron Cournot, who had written books on the philosophy of hygiene, good flesh had never been able to grow on those obsolete bones. Bichette Cournot went through the century like a poor plesiosaur, escaped from a museum. She was passionate, but men shied away from her enormous embraces. Hence, neurasthenia. As no one paid attention to her, she always thought she was alone; at the Barbinais' table, she would sometimes scratch, over the silk of her dress, her long snakeskin breasts.

Further down, two men were talking: Monsieur Moraire and Monsieur Bremen. Both had been financiers and had greatly increased their family fortunes. But domestic troubles had ruined their degenerate nerves: cuckolds, tormented by vicious children, the Catholic stockbroker and the Jewish trader now met at Doctor de la Barbinais' sanitarium, after traveling their long parallel paths. They hated each other ceremoniously with that power of mutual consideration that Jews and Christians have for each other.

Finally, Madame de la Barbinais. She was the only crazy woman in the house. Although she ceaselessly obliged her husband to make love to her, her enormous womb still cried out hungrily. She had entered Alain's room several times, her cheeks purple, containing in her hands the panic of all her organs, for the itching which was working her womb seemed to reach her liver, her stomach. She had obscene yawns. Alain spoke to her with such a gentle friendliness that she found it a sort of sedative; tipsily she would leave his room and throw herself at the doctor again.

The doctor was a nervous warden. His big, protruding eyes rolled over cheeks hollowed out

PIERRE DRIEU LA ROCHELLE

by the fear of losing his boarders, and the goatee which took the place of his chin trembled incessantly.

All these people were eating and chattering. Alain silently stared at the carafe of red wine placed in front of him. He did not drink any: the day he had left another sanitarium, after a previous cure, he entered the first bistro he came upon and, taken with a sudden craving for something that would burn his throat, had swallowed a liter of strong liquor. The alcohol, after his long abstinence, had the effect of an oil spill. In the street, he had started screaming, insulting the crowd. He had to be taken to the police station.

"You were in Paris last night!" sighed Mademoiselle Farnoux greedily.

Everyone in the house knew that Alain had spent the night out, everyone was envious, but also and above all fearful. And this fear went as far as scandal; all these valetudinarians disapproved of Alain who played with the gods of their terror, disease and death.

"There are some beautiful people who must have been very happy to see you return," continued Mademoiselle Farnoux.

"Beautiful people are not difficult."

"You, you are difficult."

"Don't believe it."

"If you weren't difficult, you wouldn't be where you are."

Her words seemed to be imprinted with understanding and sympathy; her blue eyes, however, grew hard. If Alain had opened his arms to her, on condition of sharing the excesses, the risks they were talking about, she would have refused, because she was attached like a miser to the puny treasure of her life; but she resented him for his temerity and was almost delighted to see him paying for it, because Alain was pale and had hollow features.

"You've never been to America?" Alain asked mechanically.

"No, I barely have time to get to know our old Europe, and over there, with their brutality, they would kill me. But you, you went there, I was told that you were well-liked."

She thought that those American women must have given Alain money without even counting it; she would have counted.

Monsieur d'Averseau took advantage of this moment of musing to pay court to her; but his sour nature led him as usual onto dangerous ground.

"Have you read this morning's *Action Française*? This Maurras is absurd, naturally, but there is an article on the court of Louis XIV that really crosses the line. Some poor provincial professor there who opposes Racine's world to that of Proust. But all he has to do is read the Palatine letters: one sees the same tastes as today."

"I never read *Action Française*," Mademoiselle Farnoux replied drily, for she had retained from the plebeian origins of her family a certain hatred of far-right opinions.

"I must read it because all my family reads it," continued Monsieur d'Averseau suavely, "but I don't like it. I was just saying, the other night, to my uncle ..."

He was telling the truth—his vice or his feeble apprehension made him hate any slightly violent attitude.

Moreover he despised Maurras for being a commoner and found untimely the zeal of so many petty bourgeois for values whose glittering remains sufficed as his own adornment.

"How is the duke?" asked Mademoiselle Farnoux, who was becoming amiable again, seeing all the shiny titles accumulated by the d'Averseau family.

"Better, for now," replied Monsieur d'Averseau, satisfied to resume his ascendancy over the steelworks ... "That young man brought back a bad look from Paris; he was more handsome a few years ago."

"Still handsome enough that you keep looking at him."

"That no longer matters to anyone but you."

Alain did not feel the eyes of these people on him; these past months he had not been sensitive to the ubiquitous petty gossip around him.

Avoiding Mademoiselle Farnoux's political conversation like the plague, he pretended to chat with Madame de la Barbinais.

He met with the same sighs.

"Another sleepless night," she whispered to him in a choked voice.

"A very moderate night."

"Well, you don't look too bad. You must go back to bed this afternoon, get some more sleep. Yes, go back to bed, back to bed.

"Monsieur Brême, why do you always monopolize Monsieur Moraire?" cried the doctor across the table, who was careful to include all his companions. "We would all like to follow your discussion."

Monsieur Brême and Monsieur Moraire were both given to mysticism. Moraire's confessor had recommended to him some popular works on Thomism, and he defended himself as best he could against the attacks of Monsieur Brême, who was much better versed than himself in Christian theology and was perhaps preparing himself for a conversion at the same time as tormenting his neighbor.

Madmoiselle Cournot suddenly glanced at the two men and exclaimed with unexpected violence:

"Oh yes! That would be very interesting."

But her eyes remained blank.

Brême and Moraire were nodding their heads with importance.

These nods made Alain burst out laughing, and Bichette immediately looked at him with crazy eyes.

Fortunately, lunch was over quickly. Alain avoided the coffee in the lounge and went up to his room.

Outside, it was raining and he watched with terror as the rusty, disgusting leaves beat against his window. Alain feared the countryside, and November, in this humid estate, surrounded by a gloomy suburb, could only increase his fear.

However, he loved his room, which, despite the low light, was more welcoming than any hotel room he had stayed in since leaving his family. He lit a cigarette and looked around.

The things on the table and the fireplace were neatly arranged. In the increasingly restricted circle in which he lived, everything mattered. On the table were letters and invoices arranged in two piles. Then, a stack of cigarette packs, and a stack of matchboxes. A pen. A large briefcase with a lock. On the nightstand, detective stories or pornographic novels, American illustrated books and avant-garde magazines. On the fireplace, two objects; one, a very delicate piece of machinery, a perfectly flat platinum chronometer, the other, a hideous little statuette of a naked woman, made of colored plaster, atrociously vulgar, which he had bought at a fair and carried everywhere. He said it was pretty, but he was pleased that it degraded his life.

Photos and newspaper cutouts were stuck in the mirror frame. A beautiful woman, photographed from the front, leaned back and showed the lovely sinews of her neck stretched tightly, a fleeting mouth from right to left, the double pit of the nose, the uneven horizon of the eyebrows. A man, also leaning back but photographed from behind, offered on the contrary the range of his forehead, limited at the edge by a bushy border, surmounted by the shortened promontory of the nose. Between these two photos, a news item pasted by four stamps reduced the human mind to two dimensions and left it with no way out.

This room was also a dead end, it was the eternal room in which he lived. He, who for years had no home, nevertheless had his place in this ideal prison which was remade for him every evening, wherever he was. His hollowed-out emotion was there, like a smaller box within a larger one. A mirror, a window, a door. The door and the window did not open on anything. The mirror only opened upon himself.

Surrounded, isolated, Alain, at the last stage of his retreat, paused over a few objects. In the absence of beings who faded as soon as he left them, and often much earlier, these objects gave him the illusion of being able to touch something outside of himself. It was thus that Alain had fallen into petty idolatry; more and more, he was immediately dependent on the absurd objects that his short, sardonic fancy chose. For the primitive (and for the child) objects pulse with life; a tree, a stone are more suggestive than the body of a lover, and he calls them gods because they trouble his blood. But for Alain's imagination, objects weren't starting points, it was where he came back exhausted after a short unnecessary trip around the world. Out of dryness of heart, and irony, he had forbidden himself to entertain ideas about the world. Philosophy, art, politics or morals, any system seemed to him an impossible conceit. And so, for lack of support by ideas, the world was so inconsistent that it offered no support to him. Only solids kept a form for him.

But he was deluding himself. He did not see that what still gave them a semblance of form in his eyes were residues of ideas which he had received despite himself from his education and from which he unconsciously shaped these pieces of matter. He would have laughed in the face of someone who would have assured him that there was a secret connection, ignored or wrongly denied by him, between the idea of justice, for example and the taste for symmetry that kept his room so well. He flattered himself that he ignored the idea of truth, but he was ecstatic at a stack of matchboxes. For the primitive, an object is the food he is going to eat, and which makes his mouth salivate; for the decadent, it is excrement to which he dedicates a coprophagic cult.

That day, Alain looked more longingly than ever at everything around him. Lydia's departure had touched him, it had doubled and deepened an absence, that of Dorothy. He felt more and more trapped by the circumstances which he had allowed to arise around him. And what more terrible sign than this: a captious logic had brought him back to the milieu from which he had tried to tear himself away with all sorts of outbursts. This ensemble of tranquil lunatics, who were drinking coffee in the lounge downstairs, under the portraits of Constant and Baudelaire, was his family, found once again: his mother, steeped in a timid regret for love; his father, who reproached himself for having saved only the meager earnings of a petty engineer; his divorced sister without a job; each daydreaming in front of the other two. Years of insufficient efforts, which were not multiplied by each other, let him fall back to zero.

He was standing there, the tobacco burning between his lips, without any resources, neither outside himself, nor within.

Then the usual reaction occurred. On the bare walls that enclosed his soul, he suddenly saw, of all the rare fetishes that adorned them, only the one that summed up all the others: money. He took Lydia's check from his wallet, sat down at his table and laid it flat in front of him. He was completely absorbed in the contemplation of this rectangle of paper, charged with power.

Alain, ever since adolescence when he had first felt desires, thought only of money. He was separated from it by an almost impassable abyss dug by his laziness, his secret and almost immutable will to never seek it by work. But this fatal distance was the very thing that seduced his eyes. Money—he always had it, and he never had any. Always a little, never much. It was a fluid and furtive prestige which passed perpetually between his fingers, but which never would take consistency there. Where did it come from? Everyone had given him some, friends, women. Having gone through ten trades, he had even earned some, but in derisory quantities. He had often had two or three thousand francs in his

PIERRE DRIEU LA ROCHELLE

pocket, without ever being sure of having so much the next day.

Today he had ten thousand francs in front of him. He had never gotten ten thousand francs from anyone all at once. Except from Dorothy in Monte-Carlo, but that was to gamble. He didn't like gambling: gambling was only a pretext for asking Dorothy for money. But he played with it all the same; and lost it.

Ten thousand francs was more than his usual score, but it was not enough. It was nothing. He had two hundred thousand francs in debt to begin with; and then his ability to abruptly squander money at a party had grown from year to year.

Of course, he had always had doubts about the future, but the reality of this doubt had only recently solidified. He realized that there is a limit to borrowing, that it is impossible to impose as a rule, upon his restricted circle of malleable friends, what they considered to be the exception. He was weary of this perpetual, spasmodic and feeble pressuring, the limit of which he knew was never more than two or three thousand francs. He knew also that the main source of his credit, his youth, was at an end.

Finally, would Lydia give him another ten thousand, twenty thousand, thirty thousand francs?

In order for her to give more, he would have to leave for New York. In order to leave, he had to not start taking drugs again.

But that very evening he was going to take drugs again, since he had ten thousand francs.

Money, which summed up the universe for him, was in turn summed up by drugs. Money, outside the modestly neat clothing of the hotel room, was the night.

That was the meaning of Lydia's check, lying on the table. It was night, it was drugs. It was no longer Lydia, whom the drugs and the night erased. Intoxication in the night. And night and drunkenness, ultimately, were only sleep. He was only that: night and sleep. Why fight against destiny? Why had he been tormenting himself these last months, making himself suffer? He had been afraid; at a certain moment, he had perceived this chain of causes and effects which, returning to the point of departure, annihilated him: drugs made him lose his women and his friends. Then, without both, no more money, and therefore no more drugs.

Unless this is the last dose with which to liquidate and take leave. Well, it was about time—these ten thousand francs, a few more nights, the last. Around six o'clock this very evening, he would return to Paris and sink into the final night.

Nevertheless, he was lying on his bed, and since he had not slept long enough in the morning, he dozed off.

Three

At four o'clock Alain woke up: there was a knock on his door. It was Doctor de la Barbinais.

"I woke you up, my dear friend, I regret it, because you needed to rest."

"Sit down, doctor."

Alain remained stretched out on his bed. The return to life, after this heavy sleep, put on his face a desolation which made the doctor's goatee tremble.

"You spent the night out; it's nothing, as long as you haven't done anything stupid."

"No, I didn't take any, I was with someone..."

"Ah! Very good."

The doctor looked delighted. He was counting on women to distract Alain from drugs.

But for that, it would have been necessary for Alain to be very fond of women, and for at least one of those he knew to have a positive idea of virility.

Alain frowned in such a way that the doctor's enchantment disappeared.

"I'll start using again."

"Oh no, now look here."

"What else do you want me to do?"

"No letter from America yet?"

"There isn't going to be one."

"Of course there will. Be patient."

"I am hardly a patient man, although I've done nothing but wait all my life."

"Wait for what?"

"I don't know."

"But today you know very well what you are waiting for. You admit that you love your wife and that she loves you. When she learns that you are making an effort to break your bad habits, she will surely come to your aid."

Alain, at the doctor's instigation, had written Dorothy a letter in which he assured her that he was cured and asked her to come back to him. He relied in turn on Lydia and Dorothy, and wasn't sure of either.

"She left me because she understood that I could never give up drugs."

"But you're quitting now."

"You know very well that I'm not."

"I know that you are completely clean."

"It won't last. Tonight ..."

"But at least wait for your wife's answer."

"I'm telling you she won't answer."

Alain considered himself very low for having admitted the old man into his confidence. This kind of priest, he thought, pushed hypocrisy to the point of making himself truly good, down to the bottom of his heart, so as to be able more surely to catch his clients with a display of morality.

In fact, what prompted the doctor to give Alain advice, under the pretext of kindness, was fear. He carefully avoided taking on cases of real melancholy and confined himself to peaceful and opulent fatigue; he had only accepted the charge of a drug addict like Alain because of the dazzling recommendation of a very rich lady.

Moreover, Alain himself had immediately impressed the collector in de la Barbinais, who had seen in him a splenetic dandy of the type of Chateaubriand and Constant, and also an example of this mysterious modern youth, which he could at last examine up close. Nonetheless Alain scared him; he trembled for fear that Alain would suddenly deal him some unexpected blow. His large, fascinated eyes rolled around him incessantly. He sensed in this young man, for the moment polite and kind, all the dangerous forces which prowl through life and society, and from which he kept a distance in this asylum made primarily for himself—in which, unfortunately, he had locked himself up with his wife's frenzies. Alain was almost always affable with him, the doctor was grateful to him for that; but he was not reassured and still feared to see a flash of mockery and cruelty appear from under those deliberately heavy eyelids. He had the vague feeling that Alain could have said something to him that would have humiliated him for a long time.

Despite his medical knowledge, he had persuaded himself, for his own peace of mind, that Alain could break his habit without being forced. In any case, he relied a great deal on the effects of a good emotional environment. This is why he had urged him to write to that American wife who, moreover, would be more likely than Alain to pay for the five weeks that he had already spent there.

"Listen, my dear friend, think about it. Your letter left eight days ago. The reply could not reach you yet."

Alain sneered. The doctor, in order to move away from dismal thoughts, turned toward a future where everything was right. All the people that Alain knew seemed to him just like this one: they shrank from the reality of his being.

"I'm telling you, she couldn't believe my letter. When I married her two years ago I had already promised her that I would never touch drugs again. I wasn't completely addicted at that time; I held out for a few months, I drank. And then she saw me fall back."

"But now you're on the right track."

"You know this is my third attempt."

"The previous ones were not serious."

"I have never done anything serious."

"But you learned a lot. Now you see where that leads to."

"Yes, I would rather die than fade away."

"You know all the twists and turns of temptation, you will not let yourself be taken in again. Besides, you told me yourself, drugs no longer have any effect on you and no longer amuse you."

Alain shrugged his shoulders. It was all true and perfectly useless.

The first time he had done drugs, it was without reason: a little tart he was sleeping with took cocaine; the following year a friend was smoking opium. He had returned there more and more often. He had these nights to fill: he was always alone, he never had a regular mistress because he was absent-minded. Alcohol, which was soon no longer enough for him, had also led him to drugs. And he always fell back into the same groups of idlers. They start to take drugs because they have nothing to do, and continue because there is nothing they *can* do.

He had discovered heroin, which had surprised and charmed him. Deep down, he had believed for a time in heaven on earth. Now this ephemeral illusion made him shrug his shoulders.

He had had his first overdose, he had fallen stiff one evening at a friend's house. That was when he left for America. He had continued, however, in New York, where temptations had failed him no more than in Paris. But there was not yet perfect regularity in his habit, he could still endure interruptions; and, when he had met Dorothy, he had been able, for several months, to pay homage to her with almost complete abstinence.

But he had relapsed, and suddenly he felt a totally new hold on his being, an inexorable grip. Obligatory regularity, greater frequency, larger doses. He had started to be afraid, all the more since Dorothy had abandoned him during a trip to Europe, which had suddenly made him see drugs as an agent quite beyond his control, which for all means made his life impossible.

It was then that he wanted to get clean according to the rites, by entering a sanitarium. There he found the sense of his complete degeneracy. In the midst of madmen and under the thumb of doctors and nurses, he regressed to earlier servitudes: school and the army. He had to admit being a child or die.

And, having reached the abstract and illusory point of being cured, that is to say no longer taking drugs at all, he had finally realized what intoxication was. While he appeared to be physically separated from the drug, all the effects nonetheless remained in his being. Drugs had changed the color of his life, and while they seemed to be gone, that color persisted. Everything that drugs had left him with was now impregnated with drugs and drew him back to them. He couldn't make a gesture, say a word, go to a place, meet someone, without an association of ideas bringing him back to drugs. All his gestures returned to injecting himself (for he was taking heroin in solution); the sound of his own voice could only make his fate vibrate within him. He had been touched by death, drugs were death, he could not come back to life from death. He could only sink into death, and therefore go back to drugs. Such is the sophistry that drugs inspire to justify relapse: I am hopeless, therefore I can take drugs again.

Finally, he suffered physically. This suffering was great; but, even if it had been less, it would still have been terrible for a man whose cowardice in the face of life's harshness had long been conjured up to maintain him in the complete evasion of artificial paradise. There was no resource in him that could defend him against pain. Accustomed to indulging in the sensation of the moment, unable to form an overall conception of life, where good and evil, pleasure and pain were compensated for, he could not long resist the moral panic that physical pain caused him. And he took drugs again.

But then, the stages of the drug, through which he was passing again, had appeared to him this time, in a new, dull light. With each degree of his fall, he saw what a mediocre trap it had been. It was no longer the delight of a deception that one guesses but allows to remain hidden beneath the seductive mask of novelty: now, the overworked demon had wrecked another customer and carelessly repeated the old line for fools: "If you take a little today, you will take less tomorrow."

He who had complained about the monotony of the days found it again in the very shortcut that had seemed to offer itself as an escape from it.

He also had to ultimately recognize the narrow limits within which drugs operate. It was only a more or less high, more or less low physical tone, like that produced by food or health. "I am full" or "I am not full." It was to this completely alimentary alternative that his sensations were reduced. Through his consciousness passed only the most banal ideas, all inspired by everyday life, enveloped in a false levity. He no longer had that liveliness of humor which, long before drugs, had come to him with his first bitterness, and still less that flowering of promising reveries which, at sixteen, had given him a short season of youth.

Finally, during a summer when he had not been able to bathe, nor stay long in the open air, he had seen in full clarity the real characteristics of the life of drugs: it is ordered, domestic, cozy. A narrow existence of pensioners who, with the curtains drawn, flee from adventures and difficulties. A routine of old maids, united in a common devotion, chaste, sour, chattering, and who turn away scandalized when one speaks ill of their religion.

Terror, disgust, a remnant of vitality, the desire to get in a position to conquer Lydia or win back Dorothy and, with one or the other, money—it all gave him a supreme muster of strength. From there, this last attempt at getting clean which ended with Doctor de la Barbinais.

"You don't look to me as anguished as you were a few days ago. Do you still have those pains?"

"I don't have anguish—I am in perpetual anguish."

"If you hold on for a while longer, little by little it will get better."

Alain looked away from this hypocrite. He knew that the doctor, blinded as he was by fear, possessed at least the superficial knowledge of mediocre doctors; therefore, he was lying like a tooth puller. How could he speak of will, when the illness is at the very heart of the will?

And here is one of the great follies of our age: the physician appeals to the patient's willpower while his doctrine denies the existence of this will, declares it to be determined, divided between various determinations. The individual will is a myth of another age; a race worn out by civilization cannot believe in the will. Perhaps it will take refuge in force: the rising tyrannies of communism and fascism promise to flog drug addicts.

"A healthy and strong woman like these Americans will make you forget all that," repeated the doctor with all possible sincerity.

Alain finished by nodding his head in acquiescence; for a man cannot maintain himself continuously in the lucidity in which he sees the final consequences of his habits. He falls back into the daily chiaroscuro where he balances the progress of his actions with hopes and illusions. This is why Alain still came back for long moments to the idea that he had cherished all his youth—this youth that was ending, because he had just turned thirty, and thirty is old for a boy who has only his looks going for him—that everything would be taken care of by women.

At this moment, the obscure sense of failure that Lydia's departure left him brought him back to Dorothy.

"You know what you should do, my dear friend," continued the doctor, "you should send a cable to your wife. She received your letter which must have touched her. But you have to confirm her feeling, give her the impression that you are persevering."

"What's the point?"

However, the idea appealed him. He had always been very fond of telegrams, in which he could satisfy his taste for disastrous humor and also his easily abridged outbursts of tenderness.

"Yes, telegraph her, tell her to take the first boat. Stay here until she arrives; as soon as she is here, go with her to the South or even further. Above all, don't go to Paris, don't see all those people who have a bad influence on you."

"Bah! One telegram more, or less. It won't be my first, nor my last," he exclaimed.

Then he continued to himself: "My last, yes, without doubt, my last."

Nevertheless, the doctor felt he had scored a point, and tried to take advantage of this.

"Since at the moment you are, after all, in good shape, you must also see about your business."

"My business." Alain chuckled a little in his face. Yet there were still illusions there too from which he made his daily bread.

The doctor had consideration for Alain's absurd tastes. With spontaneous admiration only for the eccentrics of the past, from Byron to Jarry, he vaguely understood that the distance of time greatly helped him to praise things which, in close proximity, would have disconcerted him just as they had the vulgar herd of contemporaries of the time. And so, in order to never be caught off guard, he forbade himself to cast stones at anything that his own age offered him.

He stood up, and once more considered with envy the ornaments on the fireplace. He would have liked to enjoy things like that but could not; yet being able to maintain his gaze for a moment on these disconcerting objects was a result with which he hastened to be satisfied.

"Your idea for a store seems excellent to me. You must immediately set about giving it substance. All of these things will amuse a lot of people."

Among other phantom projects, Alain had thought to set up a shop in Paris or New York where he would gather all these old-fashioned, ugly, or absurd objects, which popular industry, on the verge of ending and becoming vulgar, had produced in the last fifty years, and with which the refined had become infatuated in the 1920s, taking up and forcing the much older tastes of a few artists. So Alain thought he would sell a whole motley bazaar at high prices: flea circuses, collections of sentimental or obscene postcards, Epinal prints, glass balls, boats in bottles, wax figures, etc. ...

But he had to find funds to set up the store. From who? Alain had ended all his friendships. He built up vague constructions in his head, without taking steps to give them any substance.

For example, he would interest Mademoiselle Farnoux in his future. But Mademoiselle Farnoux did not spend all her income and was strictly devoted to good works: a radical newspaper, two or three Russian émigrés and a few former servants she had grown weary of.

And then Alain feared that this fashion, which was a few years old, would soon pass. He did not know that in our composite age nothing passes and that all the old fashions continue to live, piled on top of one another. There are still devotees of the Renaissance and the 18th century at the same time as collectors of Negro masks and Cubist paintings. Others still collect the remains of the Modern Style or the Second Empire. So he could have bravely gone ahead, but he wasn't crude enough for that.

"For example," the doctor continued, picking up steam, "you should do collages like the one on the mirror there. They're psychological displays, just as there are entomological displays."

Alain sneered abruptly. The doctor turned around with dread and saw what he had feared for so long: Alain's regular face was twisted by a smirk, the deceptively healthy look that the treatment had given him was all hollowed out and dented by the nervous twitches that made the ravages of the drug reappear from under the surface.

"Don't you like my idea?"

"No."

"Strange boy! Well, I see that I'm tiring you; I will leave."

"Yes, I'm going to get dressed. I'm going out."

"What, you're going out again?"

"Yes, I have a check to cash."

"Oh, I see, that's different ... but yet you could wait. Besides, it is too late."

"That's true, but I have another appointment, for the shop, actually."

"And you will still return at dawn."

"No, no."

Alain didn't bother to pretend, and while saying no, he meant yes. He was angry with the doctor for his indulgence, which left him with the door open to death, and by his defiance he wanted to force him to show it more, to the point of complicity.

The doctor sensed this challenge and was very embarrassed; for in this peaceful asylum he had no practice in authority. The fear of seeing misfortune coming to Alain could have given him courage, but even more than his recklessness, he was afraid of Alain's irony. He didn't dare protest to him that life was good, for lack of feeling in possession of very sharp arguments.

Suddenly, without looking at him, he touched Alain's hand and fled.

Four

Alain, after closing the curtains and switching on the light, began to dress to go out. He still enjoyed rummaging through the wardrobe that was left to him from the heyday, when Dorothy and he had squandered the settlement from her first husband in Florida and on the French Riviera.

A solitary man is an illusionist. In Miami or Monte Carlo, in front of a trunk full of fine linen, he would knot a new tie while smoking a cigarette. His flasks, his brushes, a dressing gown lying on the bed illuminated the dismal hotel room with luxury. He had dollars in his pocket; the night was opening, all wines would flow, he would be liked by all and everyone.

Drugs, which isolated him from all contact, which shielded him from any test, had confirmed this fantasy in his imagination.

He chose a batiste shirt, a cashmere suit, rough woolen socks; all solid gray. Over that a tie of red background. He had stolen this tie from his friend Dubourg; he had once thought that he stole things out of playful mischief, but now he knew it was out of covetousness. He also took out thick leather shoes with thick seams. Elegance effaced until it becomes dull.

He was not in a hurry. On the contrary, he slowed down all his movements, sharpening his desire.

Besides, this desire was so abstract that it could almost satisfy itself. His debauchery would be purely mental. His taking possession of the world would be reduced to a single gesture, and this gesture would not extend to things. He would barely pull his arm away from the body and bring it back immediately: inject himself with a needle. And yet the habits of hope and confidence that are woven into life are so strong that he would pretend not to limit himself strictly to this gesture; he would go right and left, he would go to people, he would talk to them as if he expected something from them, as if he wanted to share life with them. But, in fact, it would not be. Contrary to popular belief, ghosts are as ineffectual as they are intangible.

He delayed his desire so well that it ended up hesitating.

Half-dressed, he took from his cupboard, between two shirts, a pretty little case in which the syringe had been sleeping for several weeks. He held it in his hands for a minute or two, then put it down. He was afraid. Just now he had hopelessly committed himself to his inclination, but he had also seen where this final relapse would lead him. He took his revolver from his trunk, and placed it next to the syringe. One could not go without the other.

This was not what he had wanted during his early youth.

In those days he used to talk about killing himself. But the murder he caressed with such playfulness then was a voluntary, free act. Now, a foreign and idiotic force had taken hold of this fierce vow, which had perhaps been an explosion of vitality, now purified of all pretense, and this force was pushing him with both shoulders through the monotonous corridor of illness towards a belated death. Sensing this humiliating change of rulership, he had lingered in his final asylum. He had remained, motionless, fragile, fearing to make the slightest movement, knowing that this movement would correspond to his death sentence.

And now this movement escaped him: he was going to go out, already he was knotting his tie. He lowered his hands to see himself better in the mirror, over which he leaned as into a well. The pictures on the mirror frame bothered him, he tore them off. Still water. He would have liked to fix his image in this apparent immobility, so that his being, threatened with immanent dissolution, might be attached to it.

This dissolution was already well advanced. Alain had had, at eighteen, a regular face in which there was some beauty. This beauty had seemed a promise, with which he had become intoxicated. He remembered the reactions of women when he walked in somewhere. Above all, there was something unbreakable in the broad structure of his face that he looked on with pride in the morning after a night of debauchery. He had long drawn from it a feeling of impunity. But today ...

Pierre Drieu la Rochelle

Of course, there was still the solid base of the bones, but even that seemed to be damaged, like a warped steel carcass twisted by fire. The handsome bridge of his nose had arched; pinched between two hollows, it seemed ready to break. The once decisive line of his chin, which had marked such a sure defiance, no longer succeeded in asserting itself; it trembled, getting weighed down. His eye sockets were no longer neat places between temples and hard cheekbones. Something unhealthy was spread throughout all of his tissues and made them coarse, even the flesh of his eyes. But in the yellow fat, which the difficult work of detoxification had brought to the surface, was still too much life, too much being: the slightest grin, the slightest grimace made reappear those terrible digs, that terrible emaciation that had begun, a year or two ago, to sculpt a funeral mask from the living substance. He divined, ready to reappear, that grayness, those shadows which had gnawed him so deeply until the previous July.

And in the mirror, he looked behind his shoulder again. This empty room, this solitude … He had an immense shiver which seized him in the small of his back, in the marrow of his bones and which ran from his feet to his head in a thunderbolt of ice: death was quite present to him. It was solitude. He had threatened life with it as with a knife, and now that knife had turned and pierced his insides. No one, no more hope. Irremediable isolation. Dorothy in New York, she had thrown his letter in the fire and gone to dance with a strong, healthy, rich man who protected her, who held her. Lydia, on the boat, surrounded by gigolos. His shiver was even more accentuated when he received the image of this boat sinking like a walnut shell in the dreadful November night, in the dreadful black basin, lashed by polar winds.

His friends? Those who were like him were sneeringly waiting for him to fall back to them; the others turned their backs on him, carried away, absorbed by their incredible love of life. His parents? He had long ago accustomed them not to believe in his existence. When he was still living with them, he had given them the feeling of an absence all the more confusing the more kindness he showed. They had seen him withdraw with a fierce discretion from all the ideas and all the ways which seemed to them the guarantees of existence. He had refused to take his baccalaureate, he had quietly turned his head away from all the trades, he asked them for money, not a lot, but insistently, and always a little more than they could give him, until the moment when they had to cut him off. So he had plunged without turning back into a suspect world where everything seemed foreign to them, inhuman, wicked. And when he sometimes came back to them they had no words, no feelings for this abominable shadow abstracted from the world of the living, for this stranger who looked at them with the distant and derisory tenderness of a dead man.

So he would have to die alone, at the summit of the cold paroxysms of drugs.

He went to his drawer and took out the pictures of Dorothy and Lydia to banish this solitude with images, the way a devout person touches an icon. But he looked only briefly at Lydia's.

He had met Dorothy too late. She was the beautiful, good, and rich woman that all his weaknesses needed; but these weaknesses were already used up. He had waited too long.

He hadn't known early on to pounce on women and bind them to him while they liked him, and while he met a lot of them. He had kept the habit from his adolescence of waiting for them and watching them from afar. Until he was twenty-five, when he was healthy and very handsome, he had only had brief affairs, which he ended immediately, discouraged by a word or a gesture, immediately fearing that he would no longer please, or himself not be pleased long enough, tempted by the momentary amusement of a farcical exit which would be followed, once out the door, by an intoxication of bitterness. So that he had no experience of women's hearts or his own, and even less of bodies.

When he had left for New York, the mirages were renewed. In fact, he suddenly had an easier time. A Frenchwoman, whether or not she is a whore, wants to be taken and to be kept. In return, she is ready to give herself. Prudent and profitable trading. Alain was frightened by these demands for tenderness and sensuality. On the contrary, an American woman, when she is not looking for a husband, is more easily content with a thoughtless affair. Badly educated, impulsive, generous, she is not very picky about the quality of what is offered to her in an adventure. Alain, moreover, helped by alcohol and drugs, had emboldened himself from these neglected contacts. But he hadn't learned much from them.

And so, when he had met Dorothy, his disarray had been great.

Especially since something else kept him away from women, the idea that he was making money. Very naturally attracted by luxury, he always found himself in the company of rich women. But he kept telling himself that part of their charm was their money. In the invincible isolation into which he sank deeper and deeper, this idea had been exasperating.

It became an unbearable torment in the case of Dorothy, with whom he had sincerely fallen in love: she was gentle. His scruples manifested itself in an atrocious irony which he turned against himself.

"I love you, you must be rich," he had said to her one evening.

She had answered him very seriously:

"Unfortunately I am not rich enough, and I beg your pardon."

She did not understand Alain's bitterness, because she had never known a milieu in which money was not taken for granted. The fathers worked to earn it, but the daughters or the sons do not remember that and find it natural that those of their friends or their parents who do not have it get it by the only other conceivable means: marriage.

She was confirmed in this feeling by the disdainful fantasy which gave Alain the air of an aristocrat to whom all privileges were due. Considering herself less intelligent and less sophisticated than him, she saw her wealth as her only charm. She begged his forgiveness for not having more, she wanted to lavish it on him. And in fact, she spent on him what she had not already squandered from the dowry left by a fairly wealthy first husband, as well as part of her inheritance from her father.

However, Alain did not have such great need for money. Like the common bourgeois, he had only wanted the degree of wealth just above that of his parents, which he had known in his childhood. Until then, he had only incurred small debts. But he had a false reputation to uphold and didn't want to be outspent by his wife. So they had both outdone each other, and quickly found themselves in dire financial straits. And that had added not a little to their other difficulties.

Dorothy could not understand this irony he lavished on himself, on his motives. She thought that he despised himself for loving her, she who was without spirit or imagination. She imagined that he would appreciate a modest attitude. She went so far as to be humble, which Alain took for an affectation, a clever reply to his ulterior motives, pretending to hide behind her money since that was what he wanted. He thought he was being judged, and his bitterness grew.

He could have gotten through these misunderstandings, if he could have established a sensual intimacy between them, but he couldn't. This rake was ignorant, and the feeling of his ignorance made him timid. He panicked before Dorothy's modesty, which was nothing but fearful expectation since her first husband had been brutal to her and forced her into a virginal slumber. Alain took her in his arms with an awkwardness which suddenly revealed to himself the incredible poverty of his life. He didn't know what to do, because he had never done anything. He spent whole nights beside her, shivering in misery. Of course she was his wife, but for such short-lived, stray moments. He would have had to cry, to let out an immense and sordid confession; but he could not. So he grew irritable, he gritted his teeth. And this was the reason he returned to drugs, to forget the shame that had invaded him.

Little by little Dorothy became terrified. She saw herself broken, without compensation. After two or three false starts which had ended with returns of tenderness and pity, she managed to escape.

And Alain had let end this relationship, which had been the genuine chance of his life, because the drugs which had taken him over had dampened all his fears, and also encouraged him to nourish new and vague hopes around Lydia, who had appeared around this time.

But now he knew the real value of Dorothy. Deep down, he believed that he had retained some power over her and that he could take her back, if at last he made an effort. And he couldn't believe that this stir of emotion he felt was not shared. She looked so good, in this photo. Her mouth repeated what her eyes were saying: shy tenderness. Her frail breasts said the same thing, and her skin, fleeing under his fingers, her brittle hands.

He had to send her a message. He did not want death as it was now imposed on him; he didn't want to come undone sinew by sinew.

He ripped off his tie and shirt, wrapped himself in his dressing gown, and sat down at the table. He took a sheet of paper and placed it in front of him with the precision that he brought to those rare small gestures which were all that remained to him of life, and also with that fearful slowness of those who have neither the ease nor the habit of writing.

He began to make drafts:

Cable reply, need you. Minutes count.

No, not that, too tragic.

You have a lover in Paris.

Nor that, after all that had happened. He remembered that one evening, during a stay in Paris, he had gone out alone, and had run to a brothel in search of some chimerical compensation for the abstraction of his married life. When he returned, she was in the room while he was undressing and this is what struck her in the face: on each of her husband's breasts, a lipstick kiss.

This memory was so painful that it cut off his impulse. He put down his pen, discouraged, and thought about the drugs that awaited him in Paris.

Yet the white of the paper still called for his effort.

Await your letter with patience and hope.

It was flat, it seemed prudent, wise. He decided to stop there. And he copied these words complacently onto another sheet.

In all his life, Alain had never had a gesture which marked such a prolonged pursuit of the same goal. And immediately, from this sheet of paper on which this gesture was fixed, a virtue emanated. For a long moment, there was something in his life, and he was going to rebuild everything around that thing. Hang on, rebuild, hang on.

He got up, rang the bell. The maid came and he gave her the precious telegram. He urged her with feverish insistence to take it to the post office at once, and he gave her the rest of the hundred francs that he had borrowed from the porter that morning to pay for his taxi.

Then he returned to his table, fascinated. He had glimpsed the power of writing whose mesh unceasingly collects and unites all the diffuse forces of human life. He took the locked briefcase and opened it with a small key he always kept with him. There slept a few scribbled pages. On one of them was written: *The Traveler Without A Ticket*. It was the outline of a confession reduced to a few uncertain lineaments that frayed among the spaces of the paper. One sentence, one paragraph, one word. He turned the pages; he felt that fear and inhibition which froze him at the act of writing, though less than usual. He had never realized that even if his soul had not been bloodless, in order to be able to drain it he would have first had to force it, to contract it with effort and pain.

He reread a few pages which took off, hesitated, got lost. He saw the points of failure; and a little of what needed to be added to this meager text and incorporated into it, in order to live, stirred within him.

He took his pen, hesitated, grew bolder, touched the paper, marked it. A moving moment: Alain was getting closer to life. He had been taught, in certain literary circles that he had passed through in the past, to despise literature. He had found in this attitude a line of least resistance which suited his frivolity, his laziness. And besides, not truly living, he could not imagine that there was something other than what he called, with justified contempt, *literature*, and which was precisely the aimless exercise indulged in by those who had taught him this contempt. He had no idea of a deeper, necessary search wherein man requires art to determine his traits, his direction. And now, unwittingly and unknowingly, by a burst of instinct, he had entered the path at which end he could rejoin the grave mysteries which he had always avoided. Since he was experiencing the unexpected benefits of writing, he could perhaps have conceived its function, which is to arrange the world in order to allow one to live. For the first time in his life, he put his feelings in some semblance of order, and immediately he breathed a little, ceasing to suffocate under these feelings, which were simple but had become confused, knotted and tangled, for lack of being expressed. Was he not going to realize that he had been wrong to throw in the towel and conclude, without having really looked, that the world is nothing, that it has no substance?

But soon he was tired. He had completed two or three pages, he had never done so many. The little caravan of words, which carried the light baggage of desires which might have provided him with a reason for living, which he had abandoned for so long in the middle of the desert of paper, he had scarcely restarted it when he let it come to a stop and lie down again in the whiteness of the page.

As he put down his pen, he told himself he would come back to it tomorrow. And all of a sudden he was surprised, he looked at his watch, it was seven o'clock. He was able to tell himself that it was too late to go to Paris. There was a little gravity in him, he could hold on to where he was. He decided to go to bed, and have dinner in his bed, and then read a little.

His friend Dubourg telephoned him, he promised with pleasure to go to lunch the next day at his place.

Five

The next morning, around half past eleven, in a small tobacco shop on the edge of the road to Quarante-Sous, two delivery men from Galeries Lafayette had gotten out of their big yellow truck and were drinking an aperitif.

In came a man, all in gray.

He was well dressed, but his face looked odd, unhealthy. It was disconcerting to look at him, though he didn't seem a bad man.

He asked for English cigarettes. The proprietor didn't have any.

"You ought to have some," Alain said, in a cordial but nervous voice.

"There's no demand for them around here."

"Once should suffice."

"Once is not enough, the merchandise spoils."

"I would have taken the whole lot from you. But you didn't know I was coming. Give me a Pernod."

A strange conversation.

Alain went to the bar and looked vaguely at the delivery men while the bartender poured him the national drink. He downed it in one gulp and asked for another.

Then he spoke to the delivery men.

"Are you going back to Paris?"

"Yeah."

"Will you take me with you?"

"We're not allowed to do that."

"I see. But you'll have a drink with me, won't you? Bartender, two more."

He toasted with them, then they took him on board.

What was he going to do in Paris? Lunch at Dubourg's. Was that all? He would cash his check. And after? After …

When he woke up that morning he had looked from his bed at the papers on the table. But the excitement of the day before was dissipated, he had no more momentum. He had immediately decided not to write any more, to stop thinking. At the same time, he had justified his change by having lunch at Dubourg's: he had woken up late, he only had time to get dressed. He had slipped out, avoiding the doctor.

The two delivery men were intimidated by Alain, and a little frightened too, because he seemed to them to be traveling a lonely and dangerous road.

"Do you work around here?" one of them asked.

"I don't work."

"You have a pension?"

"No."

Alain gave these coarse replies in a polite tone, and so the delivery men could not say that he was mocking them.

"I'm sick."

"Ah, so that's it."

"What?"

"Well, you don't look so good."

"You could say I look terrible."

"You may have been gassed."

"Gassed? Yes, I was gassed."

"It's bad, but sometimes people get over it. I have a friend, he got it at Montdidier …"

"Let's not talk about the war."

The delivery man immediately fell silent.

All the goodwill had disappeared from Alain's face. "They're all the same," he murmured.

"What's that?" asked the one who hadn't said anything yet.

"Oh nothing. Don't you mind not having money?"

"Good lord!"

"I can't stand it."

"Obviously, if you don't work, you can't make money."

The delivery men looked perplexedly at Alain's clothing.

"You would be amazed if I told you I'm as poor as you, that I'm completely broke."

"But you seem to be doing alright."

"Yes, I seem that way."

The delivery man did not persist, and he wasn't offended because he could see that Alain was mocking himself and not him.

At the Porte de Paris, Alain got out, after giving them twenty francs. He had borrowed another hundred francs from the concierge at the sanitarium, passing the check under his nose.

They left him, happy and confused.

Alain jumped into a taxi and hurried to the Bankers Trust where he received ten beautiful new notes. Out of habit he passed by the bar at the Ritz, where he drank a martini among the sons of American families and high class pretenders. Then he had himself driven to Dubourg's.

Dubourg lived in a small apartment on rue Guénégaud, at the top of a very old house. Despite the electricity and steam that penetrated this old carcass, it was palpably rotten to the core. Alain did not like this vast staircase where a stale odor wafted and where the light shimmered in the darkness.

An old Negress came to open the door, with its wooden croak. He was immediately in the center of this bright little flat, stuffed with books, in front of Dubourg, who was customarily stretched out on the old sofa, in the middle of a pile of papers, his pipe between his teeth, pen in hand. A silent young girl was squatting next to him and watching him write. Dubourg threw down the quill, put the papers aside and stood up.

He was very tall and very thin, his bald head fixed atop a child's face, blurred by middle age.

He held out his hand to Alain with a mixture of joy and anxiety that made him awkward.

"So good to see you. How are you?"

"Eh … Hello, Faveur."

Alain kissed the girl, who stood next to her father, already tall and thin like him. She accepted the kiss with mute enjoyment.

"Faveur, leave us alone."

Faveur was already gone. Dubourg looked at Alain, looked around him, then looked at Alain again and nodded. Alain's gaze absently followed Dubourg's.

Dubourg had recently become an Egyptologist, around the same time he got married. Alain had seen, not without irony, that his former drinking companion had mellowed out. What defeat had he looked for in these papyri? What was he doing with a wife and two daughters? What was this encumbered solitude?

Yet friendship was the only opening through which some gentleness could enter Alain's heart. Alain who, with his brittle cast of mind, held the mixture of good and evil in all things to be the insult par excellence that life gave him, accepted that Dubourg got only a little of what he loved in exchange for much that he detested. Dubourg had qualities—he never lent money, he gave it; his lies were transparent; and it was with pure tenderness that he spoke ill of his friends—but he was a pharisee. Although he didn't have the manners of one, deep in his heart he hid all the imbecilic afterthoughts. It was not a pharisaism of the love of God, but a pharisaism of the love of life.

And as usual, he hastened to justify Alain's opinion; with his circular gaze, he seemed to apologize for the peaceful life that he had chosen.

But now he searched, not without effort, for Alain's eyes and, leaning his elbow on his fireplace, he asked him:

"How is everything?"

"Hmm!"

"When are you coming here?"

"In a little while."

Dubourg felt terrible about Alain's addiction and was constantly thinking of ways to cure it. Alain, in times of hope, was touched by the persistent attention of his friend and wanted to take such zeal as an example for taking care of himself. He had promised Dubourg that he would come live on rue Guénégaud, like an inmate leaving prison who wants to turn over a new leaf and short circuit his instincts. But Dubourg feared his friend's prejudice against him and, instead of confronting him head on, he lost himself in taking precautions not to frighten him.

"You will sleep here," he insinuated.

The room was welcoming. It was above the roofs of the Mint and received a lot of light. Quite narrow and very high, it was all painted in a raw white. The carpet was cream, against which the book bindings stood out, along with some fabrics, some flowers. But it was all steeped in the sweet enigma of Dubourg's life.

"Are you afraid to get out of there?" continued Dubourg, seeing Alain's pout.

"Yes."

Dubourg's wife entered and interrupted these timid approaches. She was a tall, slender woman, with languid inflections, very naked under her dress. Beautiful hair, beautiful eyes, bad teeth. She was accompanied by her two daughters—the second the same as the first—and a cat. This little troop made no noise. Dubourg had married this Fanny, he said, for her extraordinary aptitude for silence and horizontality. "When we are alone, we don't hear a sound in the house. She is lying in her room on her couch, me on mine. Only the children stand up." That was doubtful, seeing them so nonchalant.

Alain kissed Fanny's hand with great gentleness. Dubourg watched him do it in disbelief, persuaded that no one other than himself could notice the existence of a woman who was not pretty and only expressed herself in secret transports.

She motioned that lunch was served. They went to her room, where a small table was set up surrounded by stools. As in the next room, the carpet was very thick. The walls were covered with light fabrics on which were superimposed here and there pieces of Coptic embroidery, with delicate and vivid designs.

During the whole meal, consisting of two strange dishes, light and subtle, and some fruit, only Alain and Dubourg spoke. Fanny, Faveur and the other girl whose name Alain did not remember, listened with concealed pleasure. Alain felt surrounded by an insinuating charm, by a discreet plot: the cat itself joined in and brushed against him as if by mistake.

Dubourg feared that he might act up and tried to entertain him with pleasantries. He recalled stories from youth, but Alain, who had been gorging himself with the memory of his eighteenth birthday since he had reached his thirties, could not bear such a sentimental reminder from others. Dubourg however spoke with a rather humorous detachment and only used very brief anecdotes, launched with fire and then suddenly abandoned. He tried to draw comic effects from the rather brutal contrast which was impressed on Alain's mind between the Dubourg of ten years before and that of today.

At the end of the war, Dubourg was a young man, already bald, but dashing. He had a mistress who gave him a lot of money, which he gave back to other women. His apartment was always filled with easy young men and women. They drank, they made love. In the summer, they went to Spain, to Morocco. He had tired of his protectress early on; then he had caught liver disease and become indifferent about the variety of women. Early on he had had second thoughts, and they would catch him in bed, around noon, his back turned to his mistress, his nose in large books of religious history. One day, he had paid his debts, and asked for Fanny's hand, who with a nod of the head said yes. He had gone to Cairo, where she was born, and now he lived confined in absurd studies, almost poor, with the sweet vermin of woman and children on his back.

The vermin disappeared after lunch and left the two men face to face with each other in the white study, provided with coffee and tobacco. During lunch, Dubourg, while they were chatting, had sensed Alain's true feeling: he was afraid. What menaced him?

"Where are you at?"

"Atrocious moments."

"Will you hold on?"

"For what? What is there to do in life?"

Alain sat down on the sofa, right in the middle of the hieroglyphics.

Dubourg remained standing in front of him, pipe in hand. Emotions flooded in and pushed him towards his friend. The past two years, he had found a certainty, he lived in an intimate enthusiasm. But he would have had to make a huge effort to strip this enthusiasm of all that was personal, so that by letting it flow out, it would not hurt or irritate Alain. He bitterly regretted not being further advanced in his metamorphosis: one can only give what one has already completely assimilated oneself. He was too honest, and Alain too perceptive, to pretend that this work was more advanced than it was and to attenuate all the neophyte complacency that still came to his eyes and hands when he spoke of his discoveries.

Alain sensed this repressed effusion, and, without saying a word, defied his friend with his eyes. Then, an instant later, he thought of his salvation, he was terrified of Dubourg's ineffectiveness and reproached him for it in secret.

Dubourg, however, decided to put up a fight.

"Listen, there are still things in life ... well, you know!

"My dear Dubourg ..."

"A guy like you, I would like to see you do something ..."

"Do something!"

"Yes, it's marvelous, doing something well. There are two or three things you would do very well."

"What?"

"I don't know. But still, you must have some idea of your own life. And well, it's impossible that it could just perish. I hate things being bottled up; you have to get out what you have in your guts. It hurts me, *you* hurt me."

"I hurt you?"

"I'm not ashamed to say it."

"But letting out what I have inside could only hurt you even more."

Dubourg, in mid course, evaded this threatening remark.

"Whatever you do, you can do very well. You have grace, and skill."

Alain, leaning back on the hieroglyphics, shook his head. Dubourg continued to advance, fumblingly.

"Drugs aren't everything. You think drugs and yourself are one, but after all, you don't know. It could be a foreign body. There is Alain, and then … Alain. Alain can change. Why do you want to keep the first skin that you lived in?"

"To be the same. I have always been the same."

"You chose to be who you are today; you can stop being that and still be yourself, but in a different way. I know of many desires in you."

"I've daydreamed about two or three things at the same time, I didn't *want* anything."

"I know you have at least four distinct desires: women, money, friendship and then … no, that's only three."

"I've never coveted anything except money, like everyone else."

"If that were true, you would have worked or thieved. No, what you call money is the opposite of money, it is a pretext for reverie."

Dubourg paused for a moment and took a rather too obvious pleasure in the sequence of his reflections. His eyes were gleaming.

"Basically, you are a bourgeois."

"Please, let's not use words that mean nothing."

"The explanations relate only to the little things, I know that. But they have precisely the advantage of clearing away these little things."

"Go on … I don't want to deprive you of your pleasure."

"My friend, you're wrong. Psychology has not been enough for me for a long time; what I like about men is not so much their passions themselves, but those beings that come out of their passions and who are as strong as they are, the ideas, the gods. The gods are born with men, die with men, but these entangled races roll in the eternal. But let's not talk about that … You see, this is what I think: you were born of an old petty bourgeois family for whom money was a modest spring in the back of the garden, necessary to water an entirely interior culture. You had to be able to look after yourself quietly: therefore, inheritance, sinecure or marriage. Well, you who revolted against your family, you naturally inherited this prejudice. You didn't give in to the times as most around us do: you did not accept the new forced labor law and you're stuck on the tradition of money falling from the sky. But this makes you a hollow dreamer. There."

"You finished?"

Dubourg lowered his head and drew on his pipe sheepishly. It wasn't at all what he wanted to say. He should have gone much further, but it would have lasted a long time, and, despite the gravity of the situation, he still feared Alain's mockery.

"You think these explanations are futile. But you will grant me that money has in your imagination an importance out of proportion with the real taste that you have for it."

Alain did not answer, he was bored. Dubourg busied himself with relighting his pipe, which had gone out.

"Finally, there is the sun," he said suddenly.

This was better. For an instant, Dubourg seemed luminous to Alain, as he remembered that horrible summer when he had seen himself, in full clarity, exiled to a region of shadows. The drugs had brought their shadow back to his face, to his hands; he felt darkness in his eyes.

"You should come with us to Egypt this winter."

Dubourg enveloped himself in a cloud of smoke and raised a bolder eye to Alain. He remembered that he had established his balance sheet: he liked meat, vegetables, fruit, tobacco. Formerly he had become entangled in irony, but now he let his love extend to all forms of Nature and Society. This love of forms made him both worship the gods of Egypt and support his family of vermin.

"Come with us, people there have the sun in their bellies."

He continued to be unhappy with himself. He couldn't find anything direct or penetrating to say. He was beating around the bush. He returned to the charge again, but weakly. He kept repeating himself.

"You're funny, Dubourg. Nice."

Alain watched him flinch, and despised him for not asserting himself: perhaps he would have liked to be confronted head-on. Last summer,

Dubourg wrote him a letter which had castigated him. "After all, I wonder if I can forgive you for lying to me like you always do. Every time you're going to take a shot, you tell me you're going to the bathroom." Such a sentence had thrown him towards the sanitarium.

Dubourg had felt himself give way and he had seen that Alain noticed it; he gave a start.

"Look, it's not just me. There are those who live more broadly than me and whose words could have more effect on you."

Dubourg was afraid of the difficulty of making Alain understand that since he seemed to live less, he lived more. He would have liked to direct him to other examples easier to grasp than his own, examples of the open air, raw force. But, at the same time, he was indignant that Alain had no idea of the powers of the inner life, that they can blaze in the sun just as well as exploits. He would have liked to recite to him some of those Egyptian prayers swollen with the plenitude of being, where spiritual life, bursting forth, pours out all the sap of the earth. He was growing impatient and already the condemnations on his lips were on the point of turning into sarcasm. "Don't blame your poverty on life." But it was pushing him into nothingness, into hell.

However, he said:

"Listen, you're wrong about me, don't be fooled by appearances. You think you see a resigned petty bourgeois here. But I live much more intensely than when I was drunk and sleeping around. I will end with writing a book in which there will be all the virtue of Egypt. It is already running through my veins. And from my veins it will flow into the veins of other beings. We shall all rejoice."

Alain shrugged his shoulders. He exercised two contradictory prejudices against Dubourg: on the one hand, he reproached him for his optimism —for Alain, optimism was confused with vulgarity or hypocrisy; on the other hand, life, for him, could only be a gesture and not a thought. He had no idea that life could take its sources in discreet enclosures like this apartment on the rue Guénégaud. So he couldn't help replying:

"You don't seem so happy with the life you lead now."

As Alain expected, Dubourg immediately flinched. If Dubourg was strongly attached to ideas, he was not so attached to himself; which made it all the more detrimental to ideas.

"Me, it doesn't matter," he muttered. "What matters is the thought that passes through me."

"But what if you get annoyed."

"Fanny, this musty old house, it's all part of my passion."

"You no longer have the bright eyes you once had."

"I've grown old."

"So everything you're telling me … "

"No, I haven't grown old. I am no longer a young man, but I am not old. I live a lot more now than before. Here is the problem for you, it is necessary to leave youth to enter another life. I have no more hope, but I have a certainty. Aren't you tired of mirages? Basically, you don't need more money than I have."

"I hate mediocrity."

"But for ten years, you've lived in a gilded mediocrity, the worst of all."

"I've had enough, exactly."

"So, what then?"

Dubourg immediately regretted this exclamation; because it was frightening to ask Alain final questions.

"If I start using again, I'll kill myself."

"I'll stop you from that. What are you going to do in a month when you get out of here, rehabilitated?"

Dubourg made an effort to speak these words firmly and with confidence.

Alain did not dare speak to him about his boutique project.

"Business. I have some ideas."

Despite his fear of discouraging Alain, Dubourg continued to speak frankly, with a view to drawing a clear horizon.

"Listen. One of two things. Do you want freedom, or money? If you want money, you have to start your life over, enter a business at two thousand francs a month and make your way there. Otherwise, get back together with Dorothy and you can live on the hundred thousand francs in annuities that she has. You will have a small apartment like this, you will see some friends and you can rediscover your dream that you've forgotten a little for two or three years."

Alain made a face. Dubourg was astonished, then exasperated. Around what did Alain's despair revolve then?

"Alain, if you had married into a five hundred thousand francs inheritance, would you be happy?"

A glint of suicide passed through Alain's eye. Dubourg immediately felt sorry. He still wanted to resume his effort to get under his friend's skin, seize his secret reason for being and nourish it so that it bloomed.

"Listen, Alain, Dorothy is a charming woman and you are the most lovable person in the world: give the grace to your contemporaries and get back together. You are made to be tenderly served by a beautiful woman. Let there be some beings who escape this horrible pressure of work."

But this only hurt Alain, who had so little confidence in his power over women that he suspected Dubourg of feigning that confidence.

"You know very well that I have very little power over women."

Dubourg was not pretending, but he immediately doubted and his eye showed its curiosity. Yet he said:

"You're joking."

"I astonished women with the handsome face I had at twenty. Now, they still find me nice. But that's not enough."

"What?"

Alain looked at Dubourg with annoyance.

"Why are you pretending you don't know? I have no sensuality."

"You put that into your own head."

"I don't believe in missed vocations."

"Yet you're tortured by the idea of women."

"I have little control over them, but it's only through them that I can have control over things. Women, for me, have always been money."

"Nonsense. You couldn't stay five minutes with a woman you didn't like. And I've always seen you in love. You love Dorothy, even now."

"But notice that I've always been in love with rich women."

"Dorothy isn't all that rich."

"She's not poor either … "

Dubourg remained perplexed.

"So that would be the difficulty for you. You can't love a woman without money; and neither could you love a woman who has it because you have to love her money along with her."

"Perhaps … "

"But what about drugs?"

"Drugs are the solution to this difficulty."

"Yet I don't have the impression that you took drugs because you had neither a wife nor money. The proof is that you started very early, at an age when you were sure that women and money would come ... Ah! I would like to know how it all started. It seems to me that this is where I could get you back."

Dubourg wondered and fell into doubt. He was by no means fooled by the incredible cramped nature of the dilemma in which Alain was narrowing his life: the very absurdity of this dilemma assured him that it was only a pretext. And drugs were just another pretext that wrapped around that one. Did this question of when it started even matter?

He despised this childish method which unites physical dispositions and ideas in a cause and effect relationship. Physiology and psychology have the same mysterious root: ideas are as necessary as passions, and passions as the movements of the blood. So what's the use of wondering if it was the drugs that made the philosophy or the philosophy that led to the drugs? Are there not perennially men who refuse life? Is it weakness, or strength? Perhaps there was a lot of life in Alain's refusal of life? It was for him a way of denying and condemning not life itself, but the aspects of it that he hated. Why would he not give in to the impulses of his sensitivity and break, without concern for the consequences, with everything that displeased him and that he despised? Sensitivity and refinement are passions worth as much as any other. Why would he accommodate women when they are neither very beautiful nor very good? Why would he force himself to work, these tedious and mostly useless jobs which fill our cities with their futile commotion?

But then, to yield to this trajectory was to fall back into mystical protest, into the adoration of death. Drug addicts are mystics of the materialist age, who no longer have the strength to animate things and sublimate them into symbols and so undertake on them an inverse labor of reduction and wearing them down and eating them away until they reach in them a core of nothingness. They sacrifice to a symbolism of shadows, to battle against a fetishism of the sun which they hate because it hurts their weary eyes.

Not Dubourg. He was for this difficult and modest effort which is the human, and which seeks not the balance between these entities, the corporeal and the spiritual, action and contemplation, but the point of fusion where these vain dissociations are annihilated, these distinctions which so easily become perverted. If he studied the ancient gods, it was not out of a discouraged taste for the bookish, to hide from the past, but because he hoped to nourish from this study the research accorded to the inflections of his time, from this eternal wisdom. Alain, however, was thinking aloud.

"Drugs were in my veins before I could think about it."

"How so?"

"I started by drinking while waiting for women, and money. And then suddenly, I realized that I've spent my life waiting, and I'm addicted."

"But still, you had Dorothy and Lydia, and others before."

"It was too late, and besides I did not have them and I do not have them."

"Yes you do, you have Dorothy. You don't have to sleep with her for this."

"I don't have her, and that's because I slept with her poorly."

"She runs away from the drugs, that's all."

"But I take drugs because I'm bad in bed."

Dubourg was frightened by so many confessions from Alain, who usually did not like precise confidences, especially in recent years.

But, at the same time, he was thus trained to push the analysis he had started to its conclusion.

"It's funny how our lives hinge on women," he murmured.

Alain frowned. He saw that Dubourg was trying to play the cynic to lead him to a confession that would bring out remorse.

"I don't see how your life hinges on Fanny," he cut off.

"I buried myself in her warmth like a pig in its sty. And you, you need women all the more because … You've remained a child: your only link with society and nature is women."

"Yes, you told me that before, pimps are old babies. But you won't make me say I'm a pimp. You always had a pedant's taste for foul language."

Alain was becoming upset: he finally saw Dubourg's hypocrisy emerge. Dubourg wanted to force him to define himself and to settle down in that definition.

Indeed, Dubourg went on:

"My old friend, I know very well that you find me oafish, but you shouldn't be afraid to take advantage of my oafishness. I would like you to confess your immorality; which is very different from playing the immoralist. You are horribly constrained in your current conduct by prejudices —prejudices which, moreover, you laugh at."

"Wrong, I never make fun of prejudices, precisely because I have them all. Don't try that line."

Alain stood up and walked back and forth.

Now Dubourg was upset, and sorry that he was upset. And yet, on this point, he held firm: one of the surest reasons for Alain's disaster was not to have frankly admitted what he was, a lazy man beloved by women. Alain was truly the disaffected bourgeois whom he had denounced earlier, seeing vices germinate from his prejudices, but incapable, because of his prejudices, of enjoying his vices.

But he hesitated to continue: he was decidedly unsure of his means. Everything he said explained Alain, but only explained him. Something more intuitive would have been necessary: to love Alain enough to be able to recreate him in his heart. Alain had been there for an hour and nothing had happened. He was going to go away, dissatisfied with himself and therefore more dissatisfied with life, more isolated, more distorted. No!

"Alain, tell me *who you are!* Let me understand you, know you!"

"To change me?"

"If you screamed at the top of your lungs what you are, it seems to me that you would immediately cease to be it. From you to another you there is only the distance of a step."

"Or a misstep."

Alain stopped walking and looked with sad contempt at Dubourg, Dubourg who was gentle and foolish.

"Look, you big buffoon," he said softly, "you know very well who I am."

Dubourg was speechless.

"It's true."

"And you love me as I am, and not otherwise."

"But what would my friendship be if you didn't feel it as something that wants to modify or alter you?"

An exclamation came to Alain's lips; he held it back a little, then let it go.

"I would like you to help me die."

"Oh no! Alain, I love life, I love life. What I love about you is the *life* in you. How can you want ... ?"

"Yes, you're right ... Ah! If I could have confided in you."

"Yes!"

"Deep down, I can't, you know that."

"You think so?"

Dubourg was humiliated. He knew very well that to save Alain, he would have had to devote himself to him, give him several months of his life, forget a little about the gods of Egypt and really be inspired by them.

The next moment he slipped into anger. What weakness! What absence of virility in Alain! He had come to expect charity from others. But if he had been a man, he would have wanted to lean on him, Dubourg; but not to cling to him.

"Alain, I work, I am patient and so I bring forth something from myself. Come live near me and you will see what patience is. You will start by loving what there is in you of life ... "

" ... "

Six

A few moments later, Alain and Dubourg were walking side by side between the Seine and the Tuileries. They were sad and bitter.

Dubourg saw that the opportunity to save Alain had passed. He said to himself that if he had been stronger he would have attacked Alain brutally, insulted him, devastated him. He would have shouted at him: "You are mediocre! Accept your mediocrity! Hold on to the level where nature has placed you. You are a man; by the fact of your simple humanity, you are still invaluable, for others."

But he was not up to treating a man like Alain in this way. And besides, was Alain mediocre, since he was irreplaceable, inimitable? Shouldn't he rather be praised? There was in this lost man an ancient desire to excel in a certain area of life, which applause could have rectified ...

But Dubourg immediately had to recognize that he could not go far in that direction. He could hardly admire Alain, much less approve of him. So he came back to his first regret. Unable to admire Alain, he would have had to make Alain admire him; for that, he would have had to be more grand. Through Alain's downfall, he saw his own defeat.

As for Alain, he knew that he was seeing Dubourg for the last time. Dubourg's attitude, among other pretexts, gave him every reason to die: life through him had not succeeded in justifying itself. It had shown an embarrassed face, fraught with reluctance, tormented by impotent allegations.

The two friends were walking along the Seine. The river flowed gray, under a gray sky, between the gray houses. Nature could not be of any help to men that day: the square stones softened in the damp air. Dubourg shuddered; this man who walked beside him had nothing to support himself: neither woman, nor man, nor mistress, nor friend; and the sky slipped way. Maybe it was his fault; since he had never learned to rely on himself, the universe, deprived of a nucleus, showed no consistency around it.

A woman passed them, pretty and elegant. She threw a brief glance at them: she liked Alain. Dubourg smiled and shook Alain's arm.

"You see, you want to touch her. Paris is like her; life is like her. A smile, and that gray sky opens up. This winter we will go together to Egypt."

Alain shook his head.

"Do you remember …" Dubourg began.

Alain stopped and stamped his foot.

"You're rambling."

They had frolicked ten years on the banks of this river: all their youth, for Alain all his life.

"I don't want to grow old."

"You miss your youth, as if you had fulfilled it," Dubourg blurted out.

"It was a promise. I will have lived on a lie. And I was the liar."

Saying this, Alain looked at the Parliament building. What was that cardboard facade, with its ridiculous little flag? And then, all around, this flood of cars?

"Where are they going? It's stupid," he snarled.

"But they're not going anywhere, they're just going. I love what exists, it's intense, it tears my heart apart, it's eternity."

Alain looked at Dubourg for the last time. There was something positive about that face. Unbelievable. He still had an impulse.

"Dubourg, let's go out together tonight. We'll call a friend of Lydia's, she's quite beautiful."

Dubourg looked at him, laughing quietly.

"No, this evening I will write two or three pages on my Egyptians, and I will make love with Fanny. I descend in her silence as into a well, and at the bottom of this well, there is an enormous sun that warms the earth."

"Stupefy yourself."

"I'm happy."

They were in the middle of the Place de la Concorde.

"Where are you going?" Dubourg asked.

"I must stop in at Falet's exhibition. Come with me, it's on the rue Saint-Florentin."

The Place de la Concorde was already caught in the petrification of winter: a dead asphalt on which the wind sweeps dust.

Towards the rue de Rivoli lights were coming on.

Alain thought of his winters. It was the undoubted triumph of all artifices: closed rooms, glare of lights, exasperation. The last winter. This last splash of light on his face. What was Dubourg's life like? A slow and dull death. Dubourg had never left Paris, that old, sleepy little fever. In New York at least an honest atrocity reigned. Dorothy was there, between the paws of the monster which howls and turns and loses torrents of blood from a thousand sharp wounds.

A narrow street, near the Madeleine. A tiny shop, dilated by harsh light. Dubourg did not enter this dispensary without reluctance, for he knew Falet.

Falet was in the shop; he was an imperceptible weakling. Across a spine high and thick as a matchstick hung the feeble, circumflex arc of his shoulders. Somewhere above, a little gray skin, false teeth, sardine eyes. This fetus had come out of its mother's womb dead, but it had been called back to life by the bite of a snake which had left it with its venom. In the days of his youth when his door was always open, Dubourg had welcomed Falet, who in return had pierced everyone's mind with his dirty little sting.

Dubourg nodded vaguely, turned his back, and looked at the walls. Everything Falet did was business, but it was all a sham. Like the beggar in the street: all his gestures are aimed at the passer-by to seduce and entice him, but it's only a matter of getting two cents of attention so as not to fall into nothingness.

The refined were satisfied with Falet because they could place him: he was a photographer.

In the art of photography, one can only obtain the truth by force of deception; but these deceptions are delicate, they correct and cancel one another to isolate an indestructible residue. However, Falet the photographer could not get rid of the frenzy of Falet the slanderer. He made monsters of all his models; he deformed them according to a sardonic cliché, by bringing out from their faces and bodies an emphatic, improbable ugliness. Finally, under his fingers, rendered clumsy by a haggard wickedness, nothing remained of reality.

But the people of the world who are semi-intellectuals by force of being stuffed with spectacles and gossip, the intellectuals who become people of the world by dint of thoughtlessness and routine, all the Parisian rabble said they were delighted with this new excess, this new weakness.

Dubourg gazed at this museum of horrors calmly. He remembered with astonishment the time when such pettiness still annoyed him: he was used to vermin, he no longer scratched himself. Still less did he grant indulgence to the cleverness of pretenders such as Falet, who concealed his subversive efforts under a clever layer of elegance and moderation. This made the ladies wandering here and there say: "How ravishing!"

Dubourg shook Alain's hand and left.

Seven

Alain found himself alone. The barrier that Dubourg had erected between himself and death, a barrier of words, departed as after a music hall number, the stage prop along with the magician.

Falet had had a strong presentiment when he saw Alain enter; he had no doubts when he saw him stay: the comedy of rehab was over. Once before Alain had disappeared and then returned. He was coming back for good.

Alain was not looking at Falet but walking back and forth in front of the photos. He fumbled a compliment, then looked at Falet who was looking at him.

"Are you still there?"

"No, I'm not there anymore."

"Oh yes … You look good. My compliments!"

"You don't look any more like a corpse than usual."

"You choose your relationships; you like healthy people, you're with Dubourg again. That idiot, that simpleton Dubourg."

At this moment a woman entered. A drifting statue. Escaped from the hands of a Pygmalion who only a copyist, she had the ceremonial beauty of relics. Her shoulders, her breasts, her thighs had the weak excess, the redundancy of a sculpture from a late period.

Eva Canning, born in the Orient, had been raised in London. Nothing could demoralize Alain like this enormous stature. He saw too much resemblance between this illusory power, this displacement of air and his empty feeling for things.

This apparition hastened his day. This woman of a thousand favors—beauty, health, wealth—looked at little Falet with a humble and pleading air.

"We're going to my place, with Eva. Are you coming with us?" asked Falet quietly.

"Yes."

They got into Eva's car, a powerful, gentle, indifferent machine.

During the short trip, while the other two chatted indiscriminately, Alain thought of nothing, or rather thought of everything, but he saw all his thoughts caught in a devouring whirlwind; he listened within himself to the increasing speed of his fall, of his loss.

Up a steep staircase, somewhere in Montmartre, they went up to Falet's. They found themselves in an empty, freezing studio. In one corner there was a camera and a projector; in another, a few tattered books. Through a door one entered a small room entirely occupied by a collapsed sofa.

"It's cold," said Eva.

"My dear, the stove you gave me is being repaired."

This meant that Falet needed money: Eva looked ashamed.

"I'll get the blanket from the car," said Alain.

"How nice you are."

When Alain came up with a huge odorous weight on his shoulder, the other two were already installed on the couch on either side of the opium tray.

"I can't smoke with clothes on," declared Eva.

She stood up and pulled her dress over her head. She also took off her slip, her garter belt, her stockings. She was quite naked, her form magnificent and bloodless, in plaster.

Alain gave a long sneer. Never had he had such an exact feeling of his impotence. For him, the world was populated only with empty forms. It was something to make you scream, to make you die.

Little Falet, while preparing a pipe, sought Alain's gaze. Eva, who no more believed in the desires of others than in her own, shut herself up in her furs, without even looking at Alain; the latter turned to Falet.

The little man's expectant grin suddenly relaxed; he pointed to a cupboard.

There was only drugs, there was no trying to get out of them, the world itself was the drug.

Alain opened the cupboard and took a vial from it. Then he took from his pocket the syringe he had brought from de la Barbinais' place. He filled the syringe with heroin, rolled up his sleeve, and injected himself.

He remained with his back turned for a moment, looking at the wall. It was done, it was not difficult. Actions are swift; life is quickly over; we soon come to the epoch of consequences and the irreparable.

Already his immediate past seemed incredible to him. Did he really dream of rehabilitating himself? Had he really locked himself in those abominable nursing homes? Had he written a telegram to Dorothy? Had he held Lydia in his arms?

He turned around, he could clearly see Eva Canning: beauty, and life, are plaster. Everything was simple, clear, it was all over. Or rather, there had been no beginning, there would be no end. There was only this moment, eternal. There was nothing else, absolutely nothing else. And it was nothingness, overwhelming.

Eva drew on the pipe that Falet had prepared for her; then she threw herself back into her furs, blowing out a little smoke. One of her shoulders, hard and polished, was gilded by the light of the little lamp. This fragment of a broken statue, in a desert without top or bottom, lay in the midst of a warm and soothing abyss.

The waves multiplied and broke one over the other: Alain wasn't returning to drugs, he had never left them. That was it, nothing more. It didn't matter at all, but neither did life. Drugs were only life, but they *were* life. Intensity destroying itself shows that there is only the identity of everything in everything. There is no intelligence since there is nothing to understand, there is only certainty.

"Commit suicide? No need, life and death are the same thing. From the point of view of the eternal where I am now, where I have always been, where I will always be.

"The proof that life and death are the same thing is that I walk around this room and I am going to telephone Praline, because I go on as if nothing had happened, and in effect nothing has."

"I'm going to make a phone call."

"I don't have a phone. Go to the local bistro."

"Very well."

He already wanted to go away, to go elsewhere. The night was beginning. The night, the perpetual motion. He had to move constantly, go from one point to another, stay nowhere. Flee, flee. Intoxication is movement. And yet one stays put.

"You're not very polite, are you leaving already?"

"My dear Falet, I'll be back shortly, I'm going to make a phone call."

He stopped for a second in front of Eva. She was no longer plaster; while she appeared motionless, she was at the height of movement.

"Goodbye."

"Goodbye, hahaha!"

Alain went down the stairs. He wondered why stairs are made. Where do they lead? Nothing leads anywhere, everything leads to everything. Rome is the starting point for all the roads that lead to Rome.

Someone was coming down the stairs in front of him. Huge crowds go up and down the stairs.

"Excuse me."

"Go on, go on, I'm not going fast."

He was a large man with a gray mustache and a pipe. Alain remembered that face; he was a sculptor, well known to those of taste; not very famous, not very rich, modest. No doubt he lived in the building. He had a fine, tender, spiritual eye; he smelled of tobacco and kindness.

But despite his slow movements, he too was carried away by the furious torrent of life, of drugs. Alain stopped on a step and looked back at the old man. He turned around and said to him:

"If I closed my eyes, your statues would turn to dust and you would be very annoyed!"

The old man stopped, a quizzical look passed through his bright eyes, and then he left.

Alain felt like crying, waved goodnight, turned on his heels and descended the stairs four at a time.

Outside, he hailed a cab.

Eight

From the taxi, Alain hurried into a bar on the Champs-Élysées. He would call from there: nicer than a bistro in Montmartre. He loved public comfort; and he resumed his rut with a morose voluptuousness. For years, every night, he had called from bars to some apartments, and from those apartments to bars.

He felt an urgency rising within himself. When vitality diminishes, what remains of it manifests itself in the haste to be consumed. He ordered a whiskey, entered the phone booth, told Praline he was coming, went out again, took his glass from the bar.

Then he looked around a bit: faces hadn't changed in ten years. In a corner stood three or four shabby, soft-eyed men who had been young before him. One had grown fat, the other had lost his hair; but they showed the same cloudy smile.

They knew Alain and disapproved of him.

"Did you see that face? Drugs."

"He married a penniless woman."

"He's finished. He was quite something, though. Richard was very much in love with him. If he had wanted … "

Alain drank his whiskey. The stares no longer reached him; he no longer bothered to please, neither women nor men; that was over.

It was here that he had taken heroin for the first time, in the lavatory on the right. They weren't made of marble then, as they were now. At that time he was with Margaret. Another American. She was young, pretty, elegant, her smile gave the illusion of a broken tenderness. She told him that she would never forget him.

Those men at the end of the bar resented him for not having joined their side. But a few experiences had given rise to a repulsion which his pretension to try everything could not overcome. Yet he liked their company, because with them, far from women, he dreamed of women all the better.

He had stood in bars, like now, for hours, years, all his youth. People looked at him, he looked at them. He waited.

He finished his drink, paid, and left. Outside were the Champs-Élysées, the pools of light, the endless mirrors. Cars, women, fortunes. He had nothing, he had all. The whiskey and the drugs chased each other and overlapped in steady waves of burning and cold. The habit. At base, a tranquil rhythm.

Abstract stages: having taken another taxi, he was not looking at anything, neither to the right nor to the left. From the city which rose and fell on both sides, only feeble, volatile evocations emerged for him, a few personal memories. Alain

PIERRE DRIEU LA ROCHELLE

had never looked at the sky or the facades of houses or the wooden walkways, the pulsing things; he had never looked at a river or a forest; he lived in empty rooms of morals: "The world is imperfect, the world is bad. I reprove, I condemn, I annihilate the world."

His family believed he had subversive ideas. But he had no ideas, he was terribly lacking in them: his mind was a poor carcass scoured by the vultures that hover over the great hollow cities. He got out of the taxi. He paid the driver royally. One thousand-franc note, a little flame among others in this consumption of everything. These ten thousand francs had to be burnt in a few hours. For this fetishist, such little things were huge and absorbed all reality in their childish symbolism: throwing away money was like dying. The hallucination of the prodigal is worth that of the miser.

He rang at Praline's door.

Nine

"I'm going to leave my old friend de la Barbinais," said Alain, stretching out in a large armchair in front of Praline's sofa.

No one said a word, at first; but the same certainty showed on three faces.

Praline raged inside: *"Why this fake attempt? He never even went off drugs, and right now he's high as a kite."*

Finally, she let out:

"What will become of you?"

She made little effort to hide her irony, and she did not deprive herself of a glance, which could not escape Alain, towards Urcel, whose annoyance she knew was as sharp as her own.

Alain replied with only a sneer. Since these three junkies were so sure of the fate he shared with them, there was no need to speak; thus they would be deprived of the confession they so longed for.

Praline, who had just finished a pipe, stepped away from the tray she shared with Urcel and, while pushing her short, tight body into the cushions, she looked at the soft fire burning in the little stucco fireplace.

The walls were bare, and the furnishings, few in number, were formed of a few rudimentary lines. It could have been a storage room full of packing boxes. A few low lamps. When she received uninitiated visitors, she would make pipes and trays disappear into the chest on which they sat, vaguely afraid, vaguely attracted by the smell that floated in the air. The initiates would watch them out of the corners of their eyes and await their departure.

"I'm not prying," resumed Praline, "but what now? Will you stay in Paris? Will you be going back to New York?"

"I should go back to New York."

"Do you need money, my dear Alain?"

When Praline got mean, she tried, by making her voice more caressing, to deceive herself.

"Well."

Praline shrugged. Another of Alain's traits that annoyed her. Why had he not done promptly and frankly the things that would have assured him his share of the goods of this world? Resourceful herself, she liked resourceful people. The drugs didn't stop her from taking care of her interests. On the contrary, more than one deal had been made near this little lamp, there, to her left.

To mark her impatience, she abruptly changed the subject:

"Do you want something? ..."

She paused for a second. Was she going to add, "Do you want to smoke with us? Do you want some heroin?" No, since he was silent, they

GHOST LIGHT

99

treated him like a hypocrite. Having marked the time out, she continued:

"… I mean, whiskey? Champagne, maybe?"

"Champagne! I remember a young lady with whom I drank so much champagne."

Alain blushed: he hadn't intended to answer like that. He had long since given up trying his hand at this art of repartee, at which he was not very good; if he had sometimes passed for a dangerous conversationalist, it was because of his blunders. An allusion to the Praline of yesteryear stirred the air in this closed room a bit too strongly. Opium dens are places where it is inappropriate to allude to the past. Praline had been as fresh as childhood. In her eyes all the images were cheerful; her lips were swollen with blood. The men came in droves to her place, but none had stayed.

"Yes, I'm no longer a young woman, but I offer you champagne nonetheless … since you are weaned from other things."

"No, whiskey."

Praline rang. An old butler came to take orders and soon brought Alain what he had asked for. This man whose hair and teeth had been torn out by syphilis walked around without looking around. What was the point? He knew what to say to the police. Besides, he cushioned his relationships because he needed Praline and her friends in high places to protect him against his immediate superiors, who were tired of the troubles that his nocturnal obscenities brought them.

Alain poured himself a glass of whiskey. There was a rather long silence.

Urcel, who had arrived shortly before Alain, was gorging himself on his first pipe, which prevented him from speaking as much as usual. But his bulging eyes, moving from his pipe to Alain, leapt out from his thin face, under his receding forehead, while from time to time his large feet stirred beneath his empty pants.

Alain avoided looking into the darkest corner of the sofa where, like a poor relative at the far end of the table, Totote, the hideous Totote, had her solitary tray behind Urcel's back.

From time to time, a slight crackling was heard; then the smell of tropical cooking spread through every nostril.

After a long draw, Urcel finally spoke. He regretted breaking the silence, which he had enjoyed as a reproach to Alain's hypocrisy; but the desire to speak was stronger with him than anything, and sometimes gave him the appearance of careless generosity.

"Rehab's a funny thing, eh?"

"Funny thing."

There was another silence. Then Totote's shrill voice was heard:

"These gentlemen are so formal."

Alain wanted to let the good apostle go on; but he was afraid he had discouraged him by the sobriety of his answer. So he dropped a sentence or two.

"Rehab. You want me to tell you about it. What for? You know it as well as I do. I remember how you suffered that year."

"And now you, my poor Alain."

The flattering tone of junkies, and underneath it the meanness of old cats.

Totote again:

"It's touching."

Urcel had made a long, painful attempt, quite ineffective, and he had taken a long time to admit his failure. And so Alain's eyes, illuminated by the desolate pleasure of relapse, exasperated him. "I am no stronger than Alain," he had to admit to himself.

He had to immediately prove the contrary; he had to show Alain the difference between them, and make him feel his power. But, to defend himself and attack, he had never imagined anything other than to please. He could only roll with his opponent in subtle debasement. What little vitality he had was manifested only in the reactions of his skin; he was a perpetual mimicry.

He began his trick of the day, he was going to adorn himself in Alain's eyes with the feelings he guessed to be dear to him. But first, he had to exorcise himself with words of a certain personal demon who constantly inflicted on him the torture of fear.

"Why pretend to quit, my God! Out of kindness, to please a few worried friends, so as not to leave poor humanity all alone in its misfortune. But we didn't wait for drugs to bring us to the limit of life and death."

This *we*, which rushed complicity and simulated equality, greatly displeased Alain. He pursed his lips and replied:

"We try to get clean so as not to die, because we are afraid of being let go by this bitch of a life."

"Yes, we are afraid," sneered Totote in his corner.

Urcel was taken aback by Alain's determined tone; yet he persisted, by standing still, without advancing towards his goal.

"If we got clean, we'd find ourselves as we were before getting hooked—desperate."

Alain took a snide tone:

"Despair is one thing, drugs are another. Despair is an idea, drugs are a practice. It's a scary practice, so much so that we hoped to stop and get clean."

Urcel, in his turn, found the *we* rather unpleasant.

"No, no," he went on in a half-resentful, half-mocking tone. "It was an illusion, a residue of that awful intoxication that is life."

Alain saw Urcel's maneuver—in order to avoid regrets and not admit a failure, he turned the situation around and denied having made an effort. How can one lie to oneself? And yet most people, because they are not lucid, easily manage to deceive themselves. But a mind like Urcel? He was intoxicated with words, and so in order to be able to talk constantly, he was never alone.

Alain, who wanted to see all this weakness emerge, was restrained and allowed only a fairly general reflection to pass.

"Let's not make ourselves more subtle than we can be. There is absolutely no way to be subtle in this world. The most delicate soul can only walk on its two feet."

Totote immediately exclaimed:

"Its two feet, I like that a lot; its own two feet, that's it."

Her poor body squirmed in the cushions.

Praline followed the game with sharp eyes. She snapped at Totote:

"Shut up, no one is listening to you. Smoke."

Urcel, who had now begun, seemed insensible to mockery and outlined his turning movement.

"We could have done something other than drugs, but we would always have needed something that satisfies our need for risk."

Alain, appearing to notice nothing, dreamed aloud:

"There are a few vices other than drugs, but none are so decisive."

Urcel thought himself approved; he repeated with complacency:

"Yes. Since we have risk in our blood ... "

It was there, he thought, that he could please Alain, talking to him about risk. And to please him was to dominate him, since it was to deceive

PIERRE DRIEU LA ROCHELLE

him. Urcel's whole life was in this sequence: he could only deceive, since he was never himself, but deceiving someone else made him feel as though he possessed him.

However, Alain burst out laughing in his face.

"Risk! There are drugs and there are drugs. Your opium is pretty tame."

"With or without drugs, anyone who has real sensitivity is on the verge of death and madness."

"You won't die."

"You don't think so?"

Alain repressed a smile that was too insolent. With Urcel, when he felt close to being seen through, impudence became audacity.

"I've always felt myself to be in this world and in another," he said bluntly.

"No! In another! How can you be in two places at the same time?"

"Has that never happened to you?"

Alain frowned in utter disgust.

"I used to believe that, when I got drunk on words, but it was a terrible joke. Nothing moves."

"Do you believe that?" cried Urcel indignantly.

"I believe it."

Urcel wanted to save the poetic prestige of drugs.

"Still, there is a kind of derangement of everything … " he began.

Alain cut him off.

"Drugs are still life; an annoyance, like life."

"No! It's life, but touched by a certain ray of light. It's a very salutary state. We know this place and the other side; we have one foot in each world."

"Ah yes, you believe in the other world."

Alain no longer sneered. He took his glass of whiskey and drank a large swig. He was not proud of so despising a boy whose light touch he had once taken for delicacy.

Urcel made a face, he felt he had gone too far. He had been calling himself a Christian for several months; but he flattered himself that he did not anger the libertines among whom he had always lived. His art had weakened; in front of Alain, he should have said the same thing but without the religious tint. Beneath the worldly tone that Alain half affected, and which shocked him as anti-poetic, he feared a moral rigor. But he could only go on.

"You're not going to quibble over the words I use," he cried, raising his voice. "I never play with words, but I use the ones that are convenient for me. I noticed one day that I was using words which were also those of the mystics: was I going to deprive myself of them? Now look, you who are not a fanatic, you who hate systems, you will recognize a fact which is not foreign to any of us: we all have, in one way or another, the feeling that we cannot put the best of ourselves, our brightest spark into our everyday life, but at the same time it isn't lost. Do you agree? This vivacity which soars in us and which seems stifled by life, is not lost; it accumulates somewhere. There is an indestructible reserve there, which will not disintegrate the day when the forces of our flesh weaken, which guarantees us a mysterious life ... "

Urcel stopped. Totote let out a groan of fury, Alain looked at Urcel with more and more malevolence.

"I have never felt anything inside me except *me*."

But just as he was about to issue a stronger protest, he stopped short. He was astonished at the new development nourished by Urcel's ruse, an entirely internal ruse which could only fool the one who used it. But, by deceiving himself, Urcel ensured his peace. He had said to himself first: "I don't get lost because I smoke, but I smoke because I get lost"—a reasoning that Alain knew well. Then he added: "Besides, my loss is only an appearance, what I lose on one side, I regain on the other."

Alain was unable to worry about what might have been more serious than Urcel's pose in such reasoning. He had no idea what it was to be a Christian: he could not imagine this need to revive, with all windows closed, what one cannot endure in the open air, this paradoxical taste for life which, having defeated it on one plane, remakes it on another.

But, in the present case, it only took a little good taste to be scandalized at the shamelessness with which a frivolous man, a schemer of feelings and ideas, settled into whatever attitude he needed in the moment.

Moreover Alain, especially when it came to other people, never scorned facts. He did not forget that Urcel chased desperately after young men. And what first gave him success with them later harmed him: he surprised them and then soon tired them with his inexhaustible chatter. The result of these disappointments was that Urcel was cold: he came to take refuge near Praline's lamp. Before that it had been the bottle. These were the facts, but hypocrisy entered the scene, called out by fear.

Alain compared Urcel to Dubourg, who was also beginning to transpose his vitality, to save what was left of it in an uncontrollable world.

Perhaps this operation is common to all men who live by imagination and thought, especially when they reach middle age. But the passion, the madness of Alain—who, however, had never lived —was to suppose that one can live on a single plane, engage all his thoughts in each of his gestures. Unable to do so, he asked to die.

However, unable to debate, he repressed as best he could the interjections that pressed into his throat: he only repeated in a low and angry tone:

"I only know myself. Life is me. After that, death. My self, it's nothing; and death is twice nothing."

Urcel hated violence; so, fearing to provoke anger, he stifled whatever came to him in the face of Alain's narrow hostility. Behind these curt words, moreover, he still felt the rigor which imposed on him. Yet he still had to speak, first to prevent a fearful silence, and also because by defending these ideas he had encountered and which suited his vices and his weaknesses so well, he was defending his own skin. So he continued with almost pleading gentleness:

"What we call life, what we call death, these are just aspects among others of something more secret and larger. We are dying at full speed to reach for something else … "

Totote stood up among the cushions like a snake that has been attacked, on its tail.

"Why are you afraid of words? Say it then, the word you keep turning over in your mouth: God."

Urcel remained with his back turned to the poor woman; but he shuddered and gave Praline a reproachful look.

Praline looked at Totote with amused contempt. Why did she tolerate this poisoned hag? Totote, thanks to her small fortune, had succeeded in keeping with her a man whom Praline had once had as a lover and who had left her. So now Praline kept this hideous beast close at hand to draw out a slow and intermittent revenge.

The man was dead. Weak and stubborn, gullible and wanting to boast of being consequential, he had mixed up several ideas which together, he flattered himself, amounted to a total subversion. Obsessed with the idea of God, he called himself an atheist, but all his fury had ended in Manichaeism: he saw double and spoke incessantly of a God and a Devil who confounded and opposed each other in turn. He believed himself to be a communist, but his thought was so shallow that he was satisfied with the idea of a revolution which would be a catastrophe without a future. He was also a sadist. Finally, he had killed himself with drugs. Totote had inherited his hatred.

She threw herself angrily into the silence that was all around her.

"After all, I should bless you, Urcel, you are the most perfect blasphemer one can meet. No one makes a mess of religion better than you. This idea of confusing drugs and prayer is delightful …"

"That's enough," Praline snapped.

After a moment, Urcel said to Alain:

"Let's continue. Nothing will prevent me from believing that we can understand each other. I sense in your taste for risk … "

His timid nature was playing a trick on him: he had felt the need to turn to Alain as if to lean on him against Totote's attack. But suddenly, he had forgotten all the precautions he had to take with him. He had just bluntly repeated a word which, from the start, had made Alain prick up his ears:

"Risk! Do you really think you are running a risk? What risk?"

Urcel tried to hide his redoubled fear under a smile of astonishment.

Alain's voice had trembled. Steadying himself after a short while, he continued:

"You have found a nice little system to put your mind at ease. Other than that, what risk are you running? You smoke? There are smokers who live to their seventies. All you risk is making yourself stupid."

Alain stopped, looked at Urcel and suddenly burst out laughing. He thought that the conversation had finally taken its complete turn: they were coming to the point of explaining this idea of risk around which Urcel had been circling for half an hour and which the hypocrite believed he could coax Alain.

Urcel, sinking back in the cushions, turned a tortured face towards the sky.

"Obviously, in the long run, living less, you will write more weakly," Alain finished slowly. "And then what? But maybe that bothers you? Maybe, after all, that bothers you a lot? That must be the risk you wanted so much to tell me about."

Alain had gone too far; suddenly Praline hissed at him:

"Easy for you to talk."

Alain shivered.

"It seems to me that you once thought of writing. Have you forgotten the satisfactions you were probably expecting?"

Alain was immediately disconcerted. And yet, when he refused Urcel the right to speak of risk, it was with cause, because for him risk was obviously something more serious than for Urcel. He had thrown himself on the first slope he had encountered, but he descended it to the end. For nothing in the world would he have wanted to hang on and stop at a pretext.

But Praline had just touched a nerve. He had often wondered: doesn't all my disgust come from my own mediocrity? Yet he remembered the brief return to paper and ink he had made the night before: he could tell himself that he should have felt possessed by an urge much stronger than Urcel's to accept prolonging his desires and his life by thinking and writing.

And besides, he knew what old grudge fed Praline's severity. He had known her when she was still trying to live. Then, they drank champagne at her place, they didn't smoke, and at dawn she would hold back one of the men who was still there. But he would flee two hours later, disappointed, for she had been unable to give him anything, having wasted everything in the coquetry of the night.

But Praline, reading Alain's thoughts, wanted to challenge him.

"Urcel is at greater risk than anyone else, because he has more to lose than anyone else."

Alain nodded, his face blank.

"He must do his work," she finished. In her anger, she forgot her usual skill and assumed an emphatic tone.

Urcel was very annoyed.

"Please, my dear ..."

"His work, what is that?" Alain grunted.

"When you have something in your guts, it has to come out. You wouldn't know anything about it."

"What you have to say you only need to say once, there is no need to repeat it."

"My poor friend, you have no sense of these things."

Alain, paler than ever, took a drink of whiskey. He suddenly looked at Urcel.

"You've been writing for a hell of a long time."

Praline was preparing to leap forward again, but Urcel suddenly silenced her.

Alain leaned back in his chair, savoring a certainty which, although bitter, was no less easy. Again, he compared Urcel to Dubourg and said to himself: "This is what keeps them alive: their work!" He became even more enamored with his idea of gratuitousness. A naive dandy, he believed that everything could be rapid, ephemeral, without a future: a brilliant trace that fades into nothingness.

Despite Urcel's warning, Praline still let go.

"You make me laugh. Like us, you will manage well between drugs and life."

Alain slowly lowered his eyes.

"Enough," Urcel cried.

He was very embarrassed at the clumsy assistance Praline was giving him.

Praline suddenly looked ashamed. Deep inside herself, she judged Urcel very well; she knew he was, just as much as she, brutally personal and very little concerned with real sensitivity. And yet she admired him for sometimes appearing so, rather successfully she thought. She felt incapable of such skills herself, and so she adopted a certain humility.

But on the other hand, she had learned from life that you should never give people the habit of stepping on you.

"Maybe it would be better if you didn't come back here and didn't smoke anymore," she sniped at her old friend.

She was immediately afraid, not of having offended Urcel, but of a prospect opened up by her words. "Opium takes away my last years of my youth, as it takes away his talent."

Nonetheless, with her old vitality, she could not stay on such a dismal thought. She recovered quickly.

"I'm joking, Urcel, you are like a salamander. Alain, ask him to show you his latest poems, they're exquisite."

"That's one way to fix everything," growled Totote.

For a moment Urcel had been feverishly preparing a pipe.

Alain got up and began to walk around.

"What a disgrace all of this," he moaned to himself. "How life knows how to humiliate us. But, before the others, I will enter death."

There was, after all, something Christian in Alain. But above this Christianity there was a man who, if he took his weakness for granted, did not, however, want to come to terms with it, nor try to make it a kind of strength; he preferred to stiffen himself until he broke.

"I'm leaving," Alain said.

He got up and went over to Praline to say goodbye. This sudden movement changed the atmosphere. "Where is he going?" they wondered.

"My dear Alain, come back to see us soon," said Praline anxiously.

"We're running out of people," Totote dropped.

"Yes, of course."

"I like you, we are old friends. Don't be sad."

"Urcel will read you his poems," Totote added.

"Goodbye, Alain," said Urcel, confusing all the feelings in a smile: coquetry and fear, hatred and love.

"He's become impossible," cried Praline when Alain had left. "Really he's a failure and an envious person."

"Don't talk nonsense," Urcel replied bitterly. "He's a very nice boy, who is very unhappy."

"Yes, that's true, he is very unhappy," Praline continued. "It will all end badly ... but he won't kill himself."

"How do you know?" hissed Totote.

They returned to their pipes.

Ten

Why did Alain go on? Hadn't he seen enough? And if he wanted to kill himself, what better time than seven or eight in the evening, when all the desires, released from work, rush at full speed through the city in a maddening whirlwind? But no, life is just habit, and habit holds you as long as life holds you. Like every day of his life, Alain continued his rounds from five in the evening to two in the morning. Now he had to go to the Lavaux's house.

Terrible to go to Lavaux's, always terrible, more terrible than ever. The house at first was too pleasant. The mother of Lavaux who, despite her fortune, had known how to enjoy life in a quite free and noble way, had the idea of building a beautiful, solid stone house with doors and windows—and nothing else. No ornaments, just the essentials. But what is necessary forms the most perfect ornament.

It was all simple and solid, and gave Alain a glimpse at each visit of something that his character or his background had deprived him of forever: the acceptance of life in a firm and frank manner.

In front of this facade, Alain stopped for a moment. He was not drunk, he had only drunk three whiskeys. He didn't really want more heroin: the mere presence of the drug, even in a small dose, was enough for him. He congratulated himself on being decently dressed for the Lavaux's, where a harmony reigned which imposed on him.

He entered the living room and reached Solange Lavaux through a group that was gathered around her.

Solange held out her hand to Alain with that smile of gratitude that she offered to all men, for all wanted and cherished her. This generation will not see another beauty so perfect, so familiar. She was as courteous as a princess not yet made arrogant by parvenus.

A warm voice rang out. The tall Cyrille Lavaux, so upright, so thin, held out his hand to Alain. His ugliness was as seductive as his wife's beauty. He surrounded her with a love so healthy, so clear, so cheerful that she seemed an even more successful creature.

Lavaux gently walked Alain among his other friends. There were three men and three women. Alain knew all the women and two of the men.

"Do you know Marc Brancion?"

"No."

"Well, that's one way of putting it."

It was indeed one way of putting it: everyone knows heroes. In the past, one saw them in the public square, now we see and hear them in cinemas. And soon, through television, their most intimate recesses will be transparent; then a total fraternity will reign.

Brancion had the face of a hero: his complexion leaden from fever and his teeth crushed by some brutal accident. One looked with great consideration at this man who had stolen and killed, because he had done it himself, which is not the habit of the masters of our age.

Alain looked at Brancion, who did not look at him.

"Would you like some port?"

Lavaux, who always had very good port, refused to serve cocktails. He kept the tradition of his mother. And his father's? ... Perhaps, but he had to choose between several fathers: a prince, a painter, an actor out of the lower classes. With good sense he stuck with his mother and enjoyed the rich mystery, the rare freedom of being a bastard.

"Dinner is served."

They went from the living room to the dining room. What was pleasant about this house was that it was not empty. Not too many things, but they were exquisite things: furniture, paintings, objects. Anything that seemed unnecessary had its secret utility; it was not like Praline's.

Good cooking, made by a country girl, well simmered and smelling of the outdoors.

Alain, seated, looked at all of them. He liked these beings from whom he was forever separated.

Except Mignac. Mignac looked too much like himself, or at least had looked too much like himself—he detested him.

Alain found himself sitting between Anne and Maria. These were Brancion's former wives; his current wife, Barbara, was seated to Cyrille's right. Brancion was to the right of Solange, on the other side of Anne. Each time he returned to France, he had to marry a woman within twenty-four hours, whom he would leave on the day of his next departure.

"He's had women, he has stolen and killed, he knows Asia like the back of his hand. He would despise me if he knew me; but he will not know me, he will never look at me.

"All these people live, they look like they are beautiful. Mignac's cheeks are full of blood, he went to bed at four in the morning, he rode two hours before noon; then he went to the Stock Exchange, where he made money. And yet I used to walk with him at night and he was as unable as I to seize hold of life.

"What are they talking about?"

It seemed like one didn't talk about anything when sitting next to Anne. Was she stupid? Pointless question. She was peaceful, she laughed easily; she had a lover with whom she was content. She had cheated on him at first, but she had gradually been absorbed by him; now she was asleep, wrapped up in the warmth of her master's belly.

Cyrille spoke loudly, laughed loudly, called out to everyone at the same time. This hour was his reason for life. He was burning through, without haste or delay, the uncertain fortune his mother had left him; he had already sold the house in Touraine. From one end of the year to the other, he celebrated Solange with his friends, this abundant and fine body, made for the sheets, this enchanted smile, an earthly enchantment.

She had one succinct moral: pleasure. But her pleasure was easily confounded with that of others. At sixteen she left her wealthy but boring family and became a courtesan. A true courtesan, capable of joy, a Manon Lescaut. Now she was married to Cyrille, to whom she had given daughters as beautiful as their mother. She had already gone through two marriages, the only weaknesses that could make this courtesan comparable to a woman of the world. She needed money, but no more than Cyrille had. Money to animate love, love to animate money. For the moment, she loved Cyrille. She always loved for a long time. O seasons! O beds!

Did she like Brancion? Brancion was better than Cyrille, better than Mignac, better than Fauchard, better than everyone.

"Brancion, my friend Alain is devouring you with his eyes," said Cyrille.

Brancion looked at Cyrille and not at Alain, laughed coldly and continued talking to Solange. Cyrille was not jealous, he thought he would keep his wife for several years; he made love well, he still had two million in front of him. After? But afterwards, his youth would be over. He would know very well how to reform himself.

"The security, the tranquility of these people," Alain repeated to himself, speechless like a child who receives the coarsest and simplest ideas from grown-ups, and forgets to take advantage of them.

What is this ingenuity worth?

To Solange's left was Fauchard, who had recaptured Maria from Brancion. Maria was Russian. A Russian peasant girl, with a face and a body carved out of solid wood. Although he was excruciatingly bald, one-eyed, badly dressed, clumsy with words, she loved Fauchard. She had refused to marry him, but remained in his house. She slept, played with his dogs and children, smoked cigarettes, ate candy. She had never opened a book and could barely write the five or six languages she spoke.

Fauchard, the son of a man who had worked a lot, had hesitated before deciding to replace his father at the head of his factories because he prized above all to spend endless hours in the secret affairs of women, and needed little money. Yet, being modest, he had not found himself exceptional enough to reject a task that seemed his responsibility. From then on, he had without complaint stifled his immoderate inclinations, and had shown himself to be punctual, capable of reflection and decision. But on the other hand, he was delighted that a woman like Maria could easily establish herself in the freedom he had refused for himself; he was one of those men whose heart, disciplined and enlarged by work, can transpose its own pleasures onto another. In this man, despite his rather dull appearance, there was a hidden elegance that appealed to Alain. But Fauchard paid no more attention to Alain than did Brancion. Alain would have liked to please all of them, except Mignac.

"In this house, I am exactly where I would have liked to live, where I should have triumphed. I would like Fauchard to like me."

But he wanted Brancion to like him as well, and also the women. And the women did like him, moreover; each gave him a gentle, indifferent smile over the shoulder of the man holding her. The Lavaux's liked him too.

"I'm liked by everyone, and no one. I am alone, utterly alone. After dinner, I'll go."

Cyrille watched him out of the corner of his eye; he had for Alain that vague concern which he provoked in everyone and which mortified him so much. But with Cyrille, this disposition erupted in trumpeting outbursts.

As he had just taken a long swig of Monbazillac—of which he had recently received a barrel and was happy to give to his friends this evening—he shouted:

"Every time I see Alain, I remember this magnificent anecdote: at seven in the morning, a policeman finds, sleeping the full sleep of the drunkard, a young man lying on the tomb of the Unknown Soldier. This young man thought he was in bed so well that he had put his watch, his wallet and his handkerchief next to the flame, as if next to his candlestick, on his night table."

Brancion turned away from Solange and asked Cyrille abruptly:

"What? ... Who is the hero of this story?"

Cyrille burst out laughing.

"It's Alain, here. Me, I think it's a very good joke."

Brancion turned his head towards Alain, calmly watched him turn pale, then returned to Solange.

Sweat beaded on Alain's forehead. To make matters worse, Solange's gaze met his. Subject to Brancion's authority, she was mocking him, without malice, without pity.

There was a silence, a tension on all faces. But Cyrille, with a flurry of gestures and words, was already vanquishing all shame from himself and the others.

From the other side of the table, Alain again caught Fauchard's pitying gaze; Mignac had the tact to refuse him his.

It was finished.

He drank. Anne and Maria turned to him gently, but all of a sudden he was drunk. Drunk with shame.

"I would have liked to be like Brancion," he said to himself in a low voice with the shudder of a small child. "In any case, whoever we are, we want the same things as everyone else, and like everyone else we have to see about taking them, and taking them from everyone else. Then you can despise everything, things and people. But not before, not before. Before, you are a cripple who spits on people who walk straight. I have humiliated and dishonored the beautiful feeling of contempt that I had. My life should be crushed."

They left the table. Passing from one room to the other, he moaned again in a low voice:

"I'm a fool."

Some stayed in the dining room while others went to the living room, the library, and Solange's bedroom.

Cyrille took Brancion by the arm and explained to him who Alain was. In Paris, Brancion remained in Asia and looked at everything from a distance, except what concerned his immediate interests to which he gave all possible care. He had the same disdainful indulgence for the personage defended by Cyrille as he had for Cyrille himself.

"If you make me talk to him I'll hurt him even more," he said quietly.

"In the course of the evening, you can find something kind to say to him."

"I doubt it."

Brancion was smiling. He wore his dentures ostentatiously; the women were not disgusted by them.

Cyrille ran to join Alain in a corner of the library.

"I very much regret having made this misunderstanding between you and Brancion. You like him, and if he had met you in Asia, he would have liked you."

"My dear Cyrille, I adore you. Nothing that concerns me has any importance. I haven't been to Asia, and it's atrocious to not exist and to walk on two feet, because then one suffers from excruciating feet. You've no idea how my feet hurt."

Cyrille couldn't help but look at Alain's feet, then his eyes moved up to his face, where the alcohol was fighting the panic. He was holding a glass of brandy in a trembling hand.

"But I will be happy," he continued, "to congratulate Monsieur Marc Brancion for the services he has rendered in Asia for the cause of … Ah! here he is."

Brancion was crossing the room to join Solange and his wife in the bedroom; he stopped abruptly.

"I want to tell you, sir," began Alain in a tone that he intended as composed, but which seemed emphatic, "I want to tell you that I do not find it funny, any more than you do, to lie down on a grave, when it is so easy to open it and lie in it. No doubt the poor man would have made room for me … "

He had gone in for a long speech, but not knowing how to get rid of that solemn tone which clung to his words, he stopped short, hoping to make up for it with brevity.

"That's all," he ended.

"I beg your pardon," replied Brancion, as if without having listened to him, "but I never get drunk, and I have a bias against stories of drunkards. Besides, I misheard the story that Cyrille was telling."

"You like hashish better than alcohol," Cyrille remarked unhappily.

"I have known hashish, and many other things," said Brancion.

"Me, I'm a poor drug addict," returned Alain. "Drugs are stupid. Drug addicts, drunkards, we are poor relatives. In any case, we fade away very quickly. One does what one can."

Alain stopped again; he was happy, he had added the grotesque to ignominy. Brancion, his hands in his pockets, was looking at a picture over Cyrille's shoulder, who was apprehensive.

"Alain," said Cyrille, not knowing what to say, "you're quite far gone."

"No, I'm not gone, but I'm going. I'll go, I'm late."

"No, you should stay."

"I'll stay, but I will go."

He turned to Brancion.

"Imagine that I am a man; well, I've never had money, nor women. Nonetheless I'm very active and very virile. But you see, I can't put my hand forward, I can't *touch* things. And when I do touch things, I don't feel anything."

He put out his trembling hand and looked at Brancion, begging for a minute's attention. But Brancion had heard the human crowd once and for all, and had closed his ears to this concert of beggars, corner hustlers, and sentimental conmen.

Cyrille was still racking his brains to establish contact between the two men when Solange came looking for him.

"Come say hello to the Filolies who just arrived."

Alain received another blow to the heart: Carmen de Filolie, the most beautiful, the richest Chilean. Another one he had let pass.

He tried to hold on to Brancion again.

"I admire what you do because you don't believe in it."

"You are mistaken, I believe in it completely; but I beg your pardon, I am going to say good evening to Madame de Filolie."

Alain found himself alone in the library. He wanted to run away, to regain the night, the street, but as he put his hand on the knob of a door which led to the staircase, Fauchard came in, along with Mignac.

He stepped back when he saw Alain alone, but Alain, without looking at Mignac, rushed up to him.

"Do you also believe in what you do?"

"My dear sir, I know that if I tell you yes, you will despise me, and if I tell you no, you will despise me."

"You don't believe in your money, but you believe in Maria, is that right?"

"I don't really like to talk about myself."

"So you don't like to talk at all."

"I like very much to listen."

"Businessmen, seated in their armchairs, sometimes listen to the lazy people talking or even singing. But I can no longer speak, I will never speak again."

"What's wrong with you?" asked Mignac with a rather affected tone.

He remembered the years of fear and abandonment when he was poor, when he had waited for fantastic miracles in the arms of a beautiful, foolish woman.

"Fauchard, I congratulate you on having found Maria," Alain began again.

Fauchard's face lit up in spite of himself: he frowned while his mouth smiled.

"In the end, you have a wife, I have nothing; you don't know what it's like to not be able to get your hands on anything."

"Come on," said Mignac.

"One has everything one wants, but also one has nothing unless one wants it. I can't want, I can't even desire. For example, all the women who are here, I cannot desire them, they scare me, they frighten me. I am as afraid in front of women as I was at the front during the war. For example, Solange, if I were alone with her for five minutes, well, I would turn into a rat and disappear into the wall."

"We'll see about that," said Mignac.

He went out and returned with Solange, then he took Fauchard with him.

Alain found himself alone in front of Solange. A woman much more beautiful than Dorothy and Lydia, much more amorous.

"Alain, dear, what's wrong? You look a little gray, and very sad. What is it? After all you're off drugs. And the beautiful Lydia? And the beautiful Dorothy? And what other new beauties?"

"They've left. They're not beautiful enough, not good enough."

"They're lovely, they adore you. Which one will you choose? Will you keep them both?"

The kindness of women towards him. He enjoyed a certain prestige in their eyes, but what prestige! He had moved some of them deeply enough, but they were so easily resigned to passing by, leaving or not entering.

"I'm finished. I can't even move my little finger."

He stretched out his drunken finger.

"You're being maudlin now."

"Oh, I'm not drunk, I can't be drunk. I can't lose my head any longer, only the guillotine could do that. I could go look around the Place de la Concorde, but I wouldn't find it."

He stopped, he made an enormous effort to pull himself together, so as not to get lost in rambling.

He had something to say to Solange.

"Listen, Solange, you understand, you are life. Now listen, life, I can't touch you. It's excruciating. You are there in front of me, and there is no way, no way. So I'll try death, I believe that will do. How funny is life, eh? You are a good, beautiful woman, you love love, and yet between the two of us there is nothing, is there?"

"It's a question of timing, Alain, between a man and a woman."

"Women are always taken."

"Oh no! I have lots of friends waiting for you."

"They wait for me so well that they forget me."

"No, they're searching."

"They're not searching, they're waiting."

"Perhaps they love love as much as I do, when it's done well."

"Ah! there you have it, when it's done well."

He spoke louder and louder, with a choppy voice and his face riddled with convulsive tics.

Cyrille came to the threshold; Solange waved him away.

"I didn't know how to take care of myself, but still, at least once, someone should have taken care of me."

This is what he had not dared to cry out to men. A supplication would still have been better than nothing. There can be great strength in real supplication.

"To depart without having touched anything. I'm not saying beauty, goodness ... with all their words ... but something human ... well, you ... you can do miracles ... Touch the leper."

"Alain."

Solange had in her heart the silly and light vanity of a young kitten, but also a firm feeling for life, a clear goodness. She realized that the moment was serious; she knew men, she knew when they were suicidal and when they were joking, she had seen so many of them roll around at her feet or in her bed. She may well have to sleep with this one, it would give him back his heart.

Cyrille and Brancion returned. Immediately all was lost for Alain, Solange's eyes ran to her husband's slender figure, then to Brancion's rough face.

"I'm leaving," cried Alain, "I have to go somewhere."

"No, stay with us, you must talk to us some more," said Cyrille with the semblance of authority his worry gave him.

But something of Brancion's will had passed into Alain. He made an effort to calm himself, to throw them off track.

"A woman is waiting for me."

Brancion looked at him for a second.

"I'll be back, but now I absolutely must go."

"So you'll come for lunch, tomorrow."

"Yes, that's it, yes."

"But no, tomorrow I won't be eating anymore," he said to himself.

He went to the library door, he saw all these men and women, sitting or standing, here and there, in a sweet smell of good cigars, chatting with majesty.

"I will throw myself into a death where I will never see them again."

He turned to Cyrille, who asked him, "Do you want to go out through the other side?"

"Ah, yes."

"Enough humiliation."

He kissed Solange's hand, who could not get away from Brancion, who said absently:

"See you tomorrow, Alain."

Cyrille went down with him to the large tiled vestibule.

"It bothers me to see you go. What's wrong? Why didn't you spend the summer with us?"

Cyrille was very nice, but he hadn't sent him a single telegram to call on him, to save him. Like Dubourg.

"Do you have some new troubles? What is it you want? If you can't do without drugs, take some. Smoke a little, it will calm you down."

"I hate opium, a drug for concierges."

"Get married."

"I am doomed to celibacy."

"Do you need money?"

"I have thousands of francs in my pocket."

"Come to lunch tomorrow, we'll talk together all day."

A long happy day with a charming friend, in a perfect house. And every day, every day. No—the street, the night.

"Goodbye, Cyrille."

"Goodbye, Alain … Alain, stay. You like us."

PIERRE DRIEU LA ROCHELLE

"Yes, yes."
The street.

Eleven

He always found himself in the street; and already on the stairs. The spirit of the staircase, the spirit of solitude.

This November night was beautiful: the cold made the city dry and empty; however, out of habit, he looked for a taxi. He walked with a hasty step which, for a man of thirty, was heavy and jerky.

It seemed to him that the evening was drawing to a close, and yet it was only eleven o'clock. It used to be a beginning, today he was wondering how to kill another two or three hours.

Finally, he found a taxi and rushed into it. He gave the address of a bar in the lower part of Montmartre. He followed his old routine step by step: in the past, after the cinema, he spent an hour there before going to nightclubs.

The world was populated with beings he would definitely never know. He would kill himself tomorrow, but he had to finish the night first. A night is a winding road that must be followed from one end to the other.

By this hour, all the women are in mens' hands: Dorothy is in the hands of a strong man, with muscles of steel, with handfuls of banknotes in his pockets. Lydia is in the hands of gigolos, each more handsome than the last, and so she is obliged to go from one to the next. Solange will soon go to sleep in Cyrille's arms, dreaming of Marc Brancion.

Women and men held each other. Men, what brutes! All the same, attached not to life but to their work. And what chores! Egyptology, religion, literature. But there are the men of money: Brancion, Fauchard. These are the real men.

"Their world is closed to me, decidedly closed. And that's where the women are.

"Against the world of men and women, there is nothing to say, it's a world of brutes. And if I kill myself, it's because I'm not a successful brute. But the rest—thought, literature—ah! I am also killing myself because I was wounded on that side by an abominable lie. Lies, lies. They know that no sincerity is possible and yet they talk about it. They talk, the bastards.

"But me, I know very well that I'm not fooling myself. If I die, it's because I don't have any money.

"Drugs? No, look. I only took one shot this evening. So? I'm only drunk on alcohol and besides I'm not even drunk. By the way, I'm going to have another shot, this heroin must be useful for something. Here I am at the bar, I'll go to the lavatory."

"The lavatory, the loo, as they say. The loo."

This is how Alain was cloistered in his cell, he who claimed to rebel against Urcel and his pseudo-mysticism. The inevitable end of a morality of disgust and contempt.

But Alain, in this place, did not confine himself to meditation, nor did he dream. He acted, he injected himself, he killed himself. Destruction is the reverse of faith in life; if a man, over eighteen, manages to kill himself, it is because he is endowed with a certain sense of action.

Suicide is the resource of men whose resilience has been eaten away by rust, the rust of everyday life. They were born for action, but they delayed action; then action returns to them in a backlash. Suicide is an act, the act of those who have not been able to accomplish others.

It is an act of faith, like all acts. Faith in the neighbor, in the existence of the neighbor, in the reality of the relationships between the self and other selves.

"I'm killing myself because you didn't love me, because I didn't love you. I'm killing myself because our connection was loose, in order to tighten our connection. I will leave an indelible stain on you. I know well that one lives better dead than alive in the memory of his friends. You didn't think of me—well, you'll never forget me!"

He raised his arm and stuck in the needle.

This bar was quite elegant and filled with shimmering wrecks: men and women devoured by boredom, eaten away by nothingness.

Alain was sorry about Solange. Until that evening, he had never thought of paying court to her, paralyzed by the idea of Cyrille's mastery. And suddenly this woman, so easy, so difficult, represented to him all he was losing. He had a terrible regret for this flesh, so real. Human beings walked and sang in a paradise, life; they were preceded by Solange and Brancion. Even Dubourg walked at the back of this procession. He thought of Dubourg, of the gray Seine, he would never see the Seine again. But yes, he was in no hurry, he still had money, drugs. No, without Solange, it was impossible to survive.

He left the bar; he called a taxi, and rushed to another bar two hundred yards away. The heroin rose in him, but as after a tidal wave—the water passes through a breach and laps what is no longer defended.

"Here, a comrade. Standing in front of the bar, like me, alone. My fellow, my brother. He will listen to me."

Milou was a good fellow, with scruples that, by limiting his weakness, emphasized it: he did not always accept money offered to him, and so gained an idea of his honesty, a deplorable illusion which concealed his worst weaknesses. He had neither profession nor family, but vague comrades here and there. He was a handsome lad, which made up for everything else, but age was advancing.

By tacit agreement, Alain and Milou left the bar to walk in the street. Milou had been struck by Alain's expression.

"You look like you've seen something extraordinary."

Milou knew that Alain took drugs, but he could see that it was something else.

"No, nothing ... I saw Dubourg, Urcel, I dined at the Lavaux's. But yes, it's true, I saw people in a way I've never seen them."

"Ah! yes, sometimes, it's like that ... "

"Sometimes, yes."

They went down towards the Opera, through empty streets.

"But it's unfortunate not to have charm," Alain went on.

"You, no charm?" protested Milou with a vivacity that spoke volumes about his candid admiration.

Alain moved on a higher plane than his; while he, Milou, only approached people in bars, Alain followed them to their living rooms.

Alain shrugged his shoulders gently:

"No, I have no charm. I am sympathetic to certain people, and to others ... that's it."

"Call it whatever you want, people like you."

"No, they don't like me. No one has ever liked me. At eighteen, when I was quite handsome, my first mistress cheated on me."

"That's normal. Everyone's a fool at eighteen."

"But it hasn't stopped since. Always very nice, but they leave ... or they let me leave. And the men ... "

"You don't like your friends?"

"Friends are like women, they let me go."

"What you say surprises me a lot."

"It's just as I tell you. I'm awkward, I'm heavy. I've tried like hell to lighten up. I had delicacy in my heart, but not in my hands."

"You pretended to be awkward to be funny, but you did it on purpose."

"That's what fools you: I felt awkward, so I tried to make fun of it. But I have never been able to resign myself to only succeeding in the clown genre."

"But you're only like that in your lost moments."

"My life is nothing but lost moments."

"But what would you have wanted to do?"

"I would have liked to captivate people, to keep them, to attach them to myself. So that nothing moves around me anymore. But everything has always slipped away."

"What? Do you love people as much as that?"

"I would have liked so much *to be* loved, that it seems to me that I love."

"Yes, I understand you, I'm like that. But between us, I don't know if it's enough."

"I have always been as sensitive as can be to all kindness: I am not at all an oaf."

"Yes, that's something. But, you know, from there to love is still a ways to go … And besides, even if we really had love in our hearts, would that hold people?"

"We are loved only as much as we love. It sounds silly to say that, but it's true."

"On the contrary, it is because we're too sensitive that people make fun of us."

"We are sensitive, but we do not want to take them. That's it, you have to give people the impression that you want to take them, and when you have taken them, that you will keep them."

Alain stopped there. He was looking straight ahead at the rue Scribe, a place like any other. He bitterly enjoyed saying the most precise words about his life. Milou looked at him and was frightened. They lit new cigarettes and left for the Madeleine.

"You're right, Milou, I've never loved people, I could never love them except from afar; that is why, to take the necessary distance, I have always left them, or led them to leave me."

"No, I've seen you with women, and with your closest friends: you value them, you keep them very close."

"I try to pretend, but it doesn't work ... yes, you see it's not good to deceive oneself, I hate being alone, having no one. But I only get what I deserve. I can't touch, I can't take, and deep down, that is my nature."

"Maybe you're right. But you shouldn't say things like that. Thinking like that turns you into a frightened animal, it makes you want to ... "

He stopped in fear, without daring to look at Alain.

"When you really have a feeling for people," continued Alain, who had noted Milou's halt and savored the moment of foreboding, "they are very nice, they give you everything: love, money."

"You think so?" Milou asked, with infantile greed.

Alain turned from the rue Royale towards the Champs-Elysées via the rue Boissy-d'Anglas. At the corner of Avenue Gabriel, they ran into a streetwalker.

"Good evening, mademoiselle."

She was an old pro, well known to johns. Alain had accepted her services two or three times, but she couldn't recognize him, for thousands of men had passed through her hands.

"Good evening, my dears," she muttered, in the voice of an old drunkard. "Looking for love?"

"No," said Alain, "we're just having some fun."

"You can take me as well. I like everything."

"You don't like anything."

"I like to please."

"Well, good night."

"Good night, my darlings. A cigarette?"

She was covered with a heap of garments of motley colors, washed out by the rain. She reeked of grime and alcohol and reached for Alain's pack of cigarettes with a rough hand. Her face was an old sunken sun.

"If you see Monsieur Baudelaire, say good evening to him."

"Baudelaire? Who do you take me for? He's an artist."

They departed.

"What was I telling you?" resumed Alain.

"That people would give you anything if you loved them."

"Yes, but I wonder, after all, if one can love them. At the end of the day they love lies too much. Everyone, everyone I saw today, they are all the same, it's like a joke: Urcel is as grotesque as Dubourg."

"No, Urcel isn't fooled by big words like Dubourg."

"Nonsense! Urcel is a man of letters, men of letters are always duped by words. If there is one thing people are fooled by, it's their profession."

"Even us?"

"Of course, us too. It's a profession of doing nothing, of course, it's well known."

"So how are we fooled?"

"By believing that if we do nothing, it's because we're more refined."

"Oh, I don't think so—I'm lazy, that's all. I'm not ashamed of my laziness, but I don't brag about it either."

"But in your heart you believe you are refined. I believe it, I can't *not* believe it. I would have liked to please people, but I lack a certain faculty. And, deep down, that faculty disgusts me."

"So what to do?"

"Ah, yes."

"Are you still using drugs?"

"And you, do you still drink?"

"I can't, I can't raise a glass anymore. As for love, it's still easy for me. I have a talent for that."

"Not me."

"Not you! I'm surprised, I would have thought so."

"I would have thought so too."

"It's the drugs that stop you."

"Explanations, you know … "

They walked along the Champs-Elysées for a long time, saying nothing. Milou was sleepy, but didn't dare leave Alain.

Alain walked without looking at anything, as he had always done. Yet the avenue was beautiful, like a broad shining river flowing in majestic peace, between the feet of the elephant god. But his eyes were fixed on the little world he had left forever. His thoughts wandered from Dubourg to Urcel, from Praline to Solange and further, to Dorothy, and Lydia. For him, the world was a handful of people. He never had the idea that there was anything else. He didn't feel enmeshed with something bigger than himself, the world. He ignored the plants and the stars: he only knew a few faces, and he was dying, far from those faces.

They slowly walked up the Champs-Elysées; they were both tired. Alain prolonged this last human contact and let empty taxis pass, any one of which could bring him home to the de la Barbinais clinic. Milou was afraid of being left alone with the thoughts that Alain had given him. The cafés were closing; they sat down for a moment on a bench and remained silent.

Suddenly Alain resumed mechanically:

"Bah! It will all work out. In a year from now, we'll be very rich, very happy."

He looked out of the corner of his eye at Milou, who immediately seized this hope, asking for confirmation:

"You think so?"

"Are you tired?"

"Yes."

"Well, good night."

Alain stood up suddenly, hastily shook Milou's hand without looking at him, and hailed a last taxi.

Twelve

Awakening. The lead which, at three in the morning, had sealed his eyelids and his limbs, dissolves in heavy layers. But immediately an idea of deliverance begins and acts in his body: *I have definitively entered the zone of death.*

I still have time. But he looks at the crumpled banknotes on his table; he doesn't feel like spending them anymore. As for the syringe, there on the nightstand, it's used up, all used up. Lastly, he can stay in bed. But Alain never liked his bed. He was not enough of a sensualist.

He is served tea, he says a kind word to the maid, who is not pretty, who is quite dirty. He tells her that he won't get up until lunch: it is eleven o'clock.

Little by little he wakes up, he emerges from the vapors of the night, he gets up. What a face! All the things are neatly arranged everywhere, in the bathroom as in the bedroom.

He sits, he pisses, he shits. He gets up, wipes himself, re-ties his pajamas. He looks at himself in the mirror. What a face! The look of the worst days has already returned. He brushes his teeth. He lights a cigarette, he thinks. He has many things to do this morning, before lunch: telephone Cyrille to tell him that he will not be coming to lunch, or to tell him that he will come; call Dubourg. Why? To tell him to come see him in the afternoon. But no, don't call Dubourg. No mail. Nothing from Dorothy. No telegram from Lydia. Ah! The circle of loneliness with its inner spikes makes itself felt again. He will have to kill himself. Yet, on the table, there are still all these banknotes to distribute. All in all, he spent little yesterday. Several more days—but for what? Where to go? Who to see? Well, there's the drugs. They're used up, slow, insufficient. Take a huge dose. He had done that several times; he had almost died. He is not dead, but he can die. To kill oneself in this way, what cowardice!

No. So then, what?

There's the revolver there, between two shirts, in the wardrobe. Yes, but it should only be touched when one has totally decided. There's still time since the decision is fundamentally made. In the meantime, there is this money. But this absence of women, this silence of women, forever. The impossibility of seeing his friends again. Hearing them repeat themselves in front of each other.

"I will get dressed. But then, lunch with Mademoiselle Farnoux and Madame de la Barbinais, the guest table, the eternal guest table.

"I can stay in my room, have lunch in my bed.

"I will go back to bed and read. There is this detective story that should be quite amusing: you can very well get absorbed for two or three hours in a detective story.

"Let's go!"

. . . .

"Sir, you have a phone call."

How long had Alain been reading?

He wrapped himself in his robe, put on his slippers and went downstairs.

"Hello?"

"Is that you, Alain?"

"Ah! Solange."

"Yes, Alain dear, how are you this morning? Cyrille is out. I'm calling to remind you that we're expecting you for lunch. Don't come too late, we can talk. Are you alright?"

"Not bad, not bad."

"Not bad, you say that in a strange tone. But you will come, yes?"

"Yes of course. You're very kind."

"I like you very much."

"You like me very much. And Brancion?"

"Oh! Brancion, that's something else, he's the opposite of you, he's a force of nature."

"Do you like the forces of nature?"

"I like them, I like everything."

"I'm not a force of nature."

"You have a heart."

"I don't understand any of this. Goodbye, Solange ... Hello ... You think I have a heart?"

"Of course."

"Are you joking?"

Alain runs up the stairs four at a time to his room.

"Solange wants nothing to do with me. Solange doesn't love me. Solange has just answered me for Dorothy. It's all over.

"Life does not go fast enough in me—I accelerate it. The curve sagged—I straighten it. I am a man. I am the master of my flesh, I prove it."

Propped up, the back of his neck on a pile of pillows, feet on the bed frame, well braced. Chest forward, bare, well exposed. One knows where one's heart is.

A revolver is solid, it is made of steel. It is an object. To finally touch an object.